A Fatal Attraction

Venus Charts a Path to Impact Earth

I0692123

By

Tony Carrucan

A Fatal Attraction: Venus Charts a Path to Impact Earth

© 2025 Tony Carrucan

All rights reserved.

No part of this publication may be reproduced, distributed, or transmitted in any form or by any means, electronic or mechanical, including photocopying, recording, or other information storage and retrieval systems, without the prior written permission of the publisher, except in the case of brief quotations embodied in critical reviews and certain other non-commercial uses permitted by copyright law.

Under no circumstances will any blame or legal responsibility be held against the publisher or author for any damages, reparation, or monetary loss due to the information contained within this book, either directly or indirectly.

This is a work of fiction. Names, characters, places, and incidents are either the product of the author's imagination or used fictitiously. Any resemblance to actual persons, living or dead, or actual events is purely coincidental.

Published by Orbitalis Press, 2025

Cover design by M A Rehman

Cover image 'Earth and Venus in space', from *iStock*, with elements of this image supplied by NASA.

ISBN: 9781764130202 (ebook)

ISBN: 9781764130219 (hardcover)

ISBN: 9781764130226 (paperback)

"I'm your Venus, I'm your fire, at your desire."

— **Shocking Blue**, *Venus* (1969)
Written by Robbie van Leeuwen

The 1969 hit song captured the seductive mystique of Venus—a planet long associated with beauty and desire. But beyond its name and luminous presence in our sky, Venus has challenged scientists with its paradoxes: nearly Earth-sized, yet utterly inhospitable; shrouded in clouds, yet intensely bright; orbitally near, yet geologically remote. Once imagined as a lush paradise, it is now known as a furnace world of runaway greenhouse effect and volatile atmospheric dynamics. This book takes that reality a step further, exploring a provocative question: what if Venus—our nearest planetary neighbour—were to change course? Not just symbolically, but actually change her orbit?

For Sabine

Table of Contents

Preface
Sisters in Space

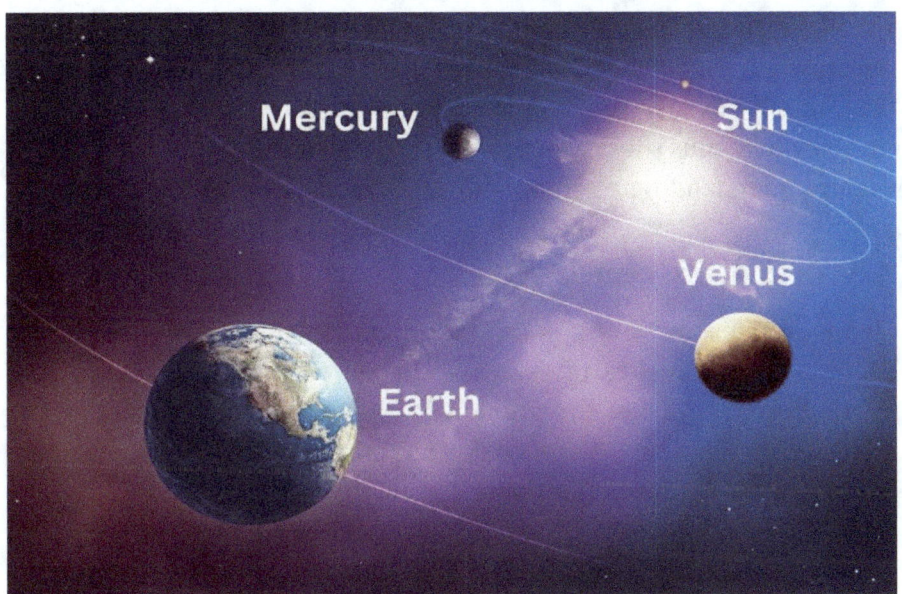

Image: iStock

Of all Earth's planetary neighbours, Venus is our closest companion in the solar system. When their orbits align at their nearest point, 38 million kilometres separate these two worlds, a mere stone's throw in astronomical terms. No other planet comes closer to Earth, not even Mars, which at its closest approach remains 56 million kilometres away, whereas Venus approaches almost twice as close to Earth.

The similarities between Earth and Venus are striking enough that astronomers often call them sister planets. Venus is nearly Earth's twin in size, with 95% of Earth's diameter and 82% of its mass. Their compositions are remarkably similar, both possessing iron cores and rocky mantles. Yet beyond these surface similarities lie stark and haunting differences.

Venus and Earth, comparable in both size and density, almost certainly formed simultaneously from identical constituents as neighbouring planets. Both planets are in our Sun's **'Goldilocks Zone'**, where a planet can potentially have liquid water on its surface. Yet both planets' current environments present a stark contrast. Earth remains water-abundant while Venus exists in extremely dry and waterless conditions. This fundamental difference raises a compelling question in planetary science - what processes expelled the water that presumably existed on Venus during its formative period? This mystery of Venus's lost water represents one of the significant puzzles in our understanding of comparative planetary evolution.

A World of Extremes

Venus rotates on its axis in the opposite direction to Earth, a peculiarity that makes the sun rise in the west and set in the east. While Earth completes a rotation in 24 hours, a day on Venus is longer than its entire year! Venus takes a leisurely 243 Earth days to complete a single turn—longer than its year, which lasts 225 Earth days. This backwards, slow-motion waltz has long puzzled scientists, hinting at some ancient cosmic catastrophe that set Venus apart from its celestial siblings.

The contrasts don't end there. Where Earth nurtures life with its moderate temperatures and protective atmosphere, Venus presents a vision of hell itself. Its surface temperature reaches a scorching 462°C (864°F)—hot enough to melt lead, thanks to the most severe greenhouse effect in our solar system. Its atmospheric pressure on the surface is 90 times that of Earth, equivalent to the crushing depths nearly a kilometer beneath our oceans.

Clouds of sulfuric acid shroud Venus, creating a perpetual veil that reflects over 70% of the sunlight that reaches it, making Venus the brightest natural object in Earth's night sky after the Moon. Theoretically if you were standing on the surface of Venus (which is an impossibility anyway), you would be overwhelmed by the smell of rotten eggs!

This brightness has captured human imagination since ancient times. The Babylonians tracked Venus's movements as early as 1600 BCE, naming it after Ishtar, their goddess of love and war. The Greeks and Romans continued this divine association, naming it after their own goddess of love. The Mayans were so captivated by Venus that they carefully tracked its movements and based many of their religious ceremonies on its appearance.

Missions to a Hostile World

For all our studies of Venus, for all our robotic missions and radar mappings, much about Earth's sister remains unknown. The Soviet Union, (now Russia), believing that Venus was another Earth-like planet with all the huge inherent material benefits, likewise expended huge resources on 17 **Venera** missions, ranging from 1961 to 1984. In Russian, Venus is called **Венера** — or Venera — a name that translates directly into English as Venus.

The Venera mission that lasted the longest was **Venera 13**. It remained operational for 127 minutes after landing on Venus on March 1, 1982. However, this mission not only provided valuable data on the surface conditions but also transmitted the first colour images of Venus's surface. The Venera program significantly advanced our understanding of Venus. Despite all the missions being destroyed by extreme conditions, they provided valuable insights into Venus's atmosphere, surface, and overall environment. To date, no other country has managed to land a probe on to the surface of Venus.

Predictably at this time, NASA also had a very active Venus program, although there were no plans to actually land a probe on the planet's surface. NASA had the following programs:

The **Mariner** missions to Venus (1962–1974) achieved the first successful planetary flybys, revealing Venus's extreme surface temperatures, dense atmosphere, and pervasive cloud cover. These early missions laid the foundation for future exploration.

The **Pioneer Venus** missions (1978) provided the first comprehensive data on Venus's atmosphere and surface. The **Orbiter** mapped the upper atmosphere and cloud structure, while the

Multiprobe delivered four atmospheric probes that measured conditions down to the surface.

Launched in 1989, **Magellan** used radar mapping to penetrate Venus's thick clouds, producing the first high-resolution global maps of the surface. It revealed vast volcanic plains, mountain ranges, and evidence of tectonic deformation, transforming our understanding of Venusian geology.

As the data from early missions revealed Venus to be a hellish world with crushing atmospheric pressure, extreme temperatures, and corrosive clouds, scientific and public interest shifted toward the more hospitable prospects of Mars. The dream of human exploration gave way to robotic missions, and Venus gradually faded from the spotlight of planetary exploration.

Over the last few decades, there have been sporadic space programs, mainly using Venus as a fly-by destination to enable spacecraft to rendezvous with other planets, such as Saturn and Jupiter.

However, current and future plans to further explore Venus are now underway by NASA, Russia, the European Space Agency and Japan.

Nevertheless, Venus serves as both a warning and a mystery. Many of its features, from its backwards rotation to its lack of a magnetic field, continue to puzzle planetary scientists. Some even speculate that Venus might once have harboured oceans and possibly life before something went catastrophically wrong!

Venus' runaway greenhouse effect offers a stark reminder of climate change's potential for catastrophic consequences here on Earth!

A Cosmic Orbit Disrupted

The Grand Tack – A Solar System Rewritten

Long before Venus ever blazed bright in Earth's sky—before Earth itself had solidified, a cosmic dance unfolded that would shape everything to come.

In the infant solar system, swirling with gas and dust, Jupiter was the first of the giant planets to form. But it didn't stay put. According to a bold theory known as the **Grand Tack**, Jupiter didn't quietly settle into its current orbit. Instead, it migrated inward, ploughing through the young disk like a ship turning hard into the wind. It approached as close as 1.5 astronomical units (the average distance from Earth to the Sun = 149.6 million kilometers), or 224.4 million kilometers, far closer to the Sun than it is today—roughly where Mars orbits now.

This mighty planet's intrusion cleared vast swathes of material, scattering planetesimals and reshaping the very architecture of the solar system. It likely robbed Mars of the mass it needed to grow large, and it churned the asteroid belt into a strange melting pot of dry, rocky fragments and icy interlopers from the outer solar system.

But Jupiter's journey was not a one-way trip.

As Saturn formed and caught up, the gravitational interplay between these gas giants triggered a reversal. Like a sailing vessel executing a **"tack"** across the wind, Jupiter turned back, retreating outward to the orbit it occupies today. Saturn followed. Together, they left behind a solar system transformed—one where Earth and Venus would emerge in a relatively compact zone of stability.

It was this cosmic upheaval—this **Grand Tack**—that may explain why Venus and Earth are near-twins in size and position, yet destined for radically different fates. One would become a cradle of life. The other, a cautionary tale written in sulphur and fire.

Planetary Orbits Are Not as Stable as We Once Thought

For much of history, scientists assumed the solar system operated like a finely tuned clockwork—planets circling the Sun in neat, predictable orbits forever. But modern astronomy paints a more unsettling picture.

Using complex computer simulations, French astronomer Jacques Laskar and others have shown that the inner planets—Mercury, Venus, Earth, and Mars—are subject to chaotic diffusion. This means their orbits slowly change over time in unpredictable ways, mainly due to subtle gravitational interactions between them.

Laskar ran over 1,000 different simulations of the solar system's future, each with slightly different starting conditions. The result? In some cases, Mercury's orbit becomes dangerously elongated, or "eccentric," increasing the risk of planetary collisions or ejections from the system. In extreme cases (about 1–2% of simulations), Mercury's orbit stretches so far that it could cross Venus's path or even collide with the Sun.

Interestingly, these instabilities seem more pronounced when relativistic effects from Einstein's theory of general relativity are left out. That's right—without the subtle bending of space-time near the Sun, the solar system becomes noticeably more unstable.

As for Venus, Earth, and Mars, their orbits also show signs of slow, chaotic drift in both shape and tilt. While not as dramatic as Mercury's fate, these variations could affect Earth's climate over geological timescales.

The lesson is clear:

Planets are not permanently fixed in their orbits – orbits can shift!

What happened once... may happen again.

Perhaps that's why the events that follow seem both impossible and, in retrospect, somehow inevitable. In all our observations and in all our calculations, we never considered that Venus might break free from its ancient orbit. We never imagined that our nearest planetary neighbour might suddenly chart a new course—one that would bring it closer to Earth than any planet has come since the solar system's violent birth.

This is the story of what happened when Venus changed its cosmic orbit and how humanity faced the prospect of a close encounter with its turbulent twin. It is a tale of science and wonder, of cosmic forces beyond our control, and of humanity's response in the face of an unprecedented crisis.

It is, in essence, the tale of a **'fatal attraction'** between two celestial bodies and the inevitable consequences that follow!

Chapter 1
It Began on a Normal Night

Image: iStock

It began on a normal night, the kind Andy loved best—clear skies, a hint of autumn crispness in the air, and no interruptions from his neighbor's overly enthusiastic Labrador. Andy had just set up his trusty (and slightly battered) telescope in his backyard, in suburban Melbourne, Australia. At this time of the year, his first target was Venus, the brilliant "Evening Star," shining like a celestial lighthouse in the western sky. Andy loved this planet named after the goddess of love, he loved the way it shone, the way it morphed into different shapes, the way it offered a promise of paradise; although Andy knew better of course, Venus was literally a hell, something that would destroy an unprotected human body in nanoseconds!

But enough of this, Andy was savoring his first look at the goddess tonight, but as he looked into the eyepiece, something about Venus seemed... well, a bit off!

Leaning harder into the eyepiece, Andy frowned, then squinted, then looked again. The planet wasn't just bright—it was too bright, like someone had cranked up the cosmic dimmer switch and forgotten to stop! It also seemed larger, more pronounced, as though it were sidling up to Earth for a better look.

"Huh," Andy muttered. "Wow!"

He recalibrated the telescope, squinted harder, and even adjusted his glasses for good measure. Still the same: Venus glared back at him, bold and unblinking. "It's probably an illusion," he said aloud, reassuring himself. "Atmospheric refraction. Something scientific and boring. Totally normal."

With that, Andy packed up for the night, chalking it up to his overactive imagination. But the unease lingered.

A Teacher's Startling Observation

Some 13,000 kilometres away, standing in her backyard observatory in suburban Phoenix, Arizona, Maria Suarez was squinting through her telescope on what should have been a routine evening of stargazing. Maria Suarez always told her students that the best discoveries often come by accident. She was about to prove her own point.

The evening had started normally enough. She'd finished grading papers from her high school physics class, made her usual cup of tea, and stepped out into the cooling desert air. She thought that she might start with Venus, as she hadn't observed Venus since its last transit through the western night sky. Venus hung bright in the twilight sky; as usual, a beacon she'd observed hundreds of times before. But tonight was different.

At first, she thought her telescope needed cleaning. The image seemed different—Venus appeared larger and brighter than it should be. She checked her equipment, recalibrated, and even went inside to clean her glasses.

When she returned, the anomaly remained. After sitting quietly for what seemed like an eternity, Maria's hands trembled slightly as she reached for her phone. She hesitated before opening the amateur astronomers' forum she frequented. Would they laugh at her? Call her an alarmist. But the scientist in her knew that data needed to be shared, no matter how unlikely it seemed.

Her post was simple: "Venus observation anomaly—apparently approximately 15% larger than expected. Equipment verified. Anyone else seeing this?"

The responses trickled in, slowly at first, then faster. A hobbyist in New Mexico reported similar findings. Another in Texas. By midnight, her inbox was flooded with messages from amateur astronomers across the globe, all reporting the same phenomenon.

She stayed up until dawn, corresponding with observers worldwide. Each confirmation made her heartbeat faster. This wasn't an equipment failure or atmospheric distortion. This was real!

The next morning, fighting exhaustion, she faced her first period physics class. The students noticed something was not quite right— Ms. Suarez was usually energetic and enthusiastic. Today she seemed distracted, checking her phone between equations.

"Ms. Suarez?" Emma, a bright senior with dreams of becoming an astronaut, raised her hand. "Are you okay?"

Maria looked at her students' young minds still full of wonder about the universe. Should she tell them? Would it inspire or frighten them?

"Actually," she said, setting down her chalk, "I want to show you something." She pulled up the forum on the classroom projector, watching their faces as they absorbed the implications.

"But planets don't just change orbits, do they?" asked Marcus from the back row.

"That's what we thought," Maria replied. "But science is about observing what actually happens, not what we think should happen."

By lunchtime, professional observatories were confirming the amateur observations. Maria's phone wouldn't stop buzzing with notifications. Her simple forum post had sparked a global conversation.

In Chile's Atacama Desert, Dr. Elena Rossi was about to end her shift at the European Southern Observatory when the first email arrived. She almost deleted it—another amateur astronomy report, probably nothing. But something made her pause. The data looked too precise, too consistent across multiple observations. She began making calls.

The sophisticated instruments at her disposal confirmed what Maria's backyard telescope had first spotted. Venus wasn't where it should be. The planet's orbit was changing in ways that defied their understanding of celestial mechanics.

Global Attention Builds

Within forty-eight hours, observatories worldwide were focused on Venus. The planet wasn't just appearing larger; it was moving. Breaking free from its normal orbital path in a way that defied every model of celestial mechanics they'd ever created.

News organizations picked up the story but initially treated it as a curiosity. Local stations interviewed Maria, focusing more on the human-interest angle of a high school teacher making an important astronomical discovery than on the implications of what she'd found.

But in the scientific community, alarm bells were ringing. Emergency meetings were convened. Data was shared, analyzed, and debated. Variables were checked and rechecked.

A week after Maria's first observation, she received a notification from the AAVSO (American Association of Variable Star Observers). Her uploaded Venus observations had been flagged by their NASA liaison program. The message explained that NASA's Planetary Science Division was assembling a distributed observation network to track Venus's anomalous behavior, and her location and equipment specifications made her an ideal contributor. Instructions followed for calibrating her observations to their protocols. Maria's heart raced as she realized her backyard observatory, humble as it was, had been invited to join a global network of eyes watching Venus's inexplicable journey.

Her students became her assistants, learning more about astronomical observation in those few weeks than they had in years of formal education. They helped her log data, track changes, and communicate with other observers around the world.

"You know what's crazy?" Emma said one evening, as they reviewed the latest measurements. "In all of human history, Venus has been predictable. Ancient civilizations could track its movements. And now, suddenly, it's doing something new."

Maria nodded. "Sometimes the universe reminds us that we still have a lot to learn."

As the days passed, the changes became visible even to the naked eye. Venus grew brighter in the evening sky, catching the attention of even casual observers. People began to ask questions, to look up with renewed interest and growing concern.

Maria's forum post had opened a door that couldn't be closed. Humanity was about to face something unprecedented, and it had started with a few people simply paying attention to something unusual in the night sky.

The amateur astronomy community, often overlooked by professionals, had proven its worth. Their global network of observers had provided crucial early warning of a phenomenon that would soon command the world's attention.

As Maria prepared for another night of observation, she thought about how many other eyes were now turned toward Venus and how many other people were watching and wondering. The universe had thrown them a cosmic curve ball, and no one knew where it would lead.

Earlier Warning Signs

Some months before amateur astronomers like Andy and Maria noticed Venus's unusual brightness and size, a handful of specialized observatories had already started recording troubling anomalies.

Nestled in remote locations, these institutions lacked the prestige of NASA or the European Space Agency, who incidentally were primarily focused on mission-based planetary studies. However, these smaller observatories maintained long-term astrometric programs, tracking planetary positions with meticulous precision.

Up in the mountains of Chile, at the Cerro Armazones Observatory, Dr. Emiliano Fuentes had devoted his life to watching the dance of planets. Year after year, he refined his models, checking them against what he actually saw in the night sky. But something was beginning to worry him deeply. Venus, that brilliant point of light we can often see from Earth, was changing its rhythm.

The time it took Venus to complete its cycle around the Sun as viewed from Earth—what scientists call its "synodic period"—was getting shorter. Normally, this cycle lasted about 584 Earth days, like clockwork. But now? It had shrunk to just under 580 days. Most people wouldn't notice such a small change, but for someone like Fuentes who measured these movements with meticulous care, this shift was as startling as finding a stranger in your home.

Meanwhile, halfway across the world in the remote mountains of Tibet, researchers at the Tanggula Observatory were puzzled by their own discovery. Venus was showing up three to four days early for its cosmic appointments. The planet wasn't where their calculations said it should be—it was arriving ahead of schedule. Nothing in their historical records could explain this change, and nobody had ever seen anything like it before.

At first, these discrepancies were dismissed as minor computational errors, artifacts of imperfect data. But as the weeks passed, the shift became undeniable. Venus was no longer behaving as expected. Some researchers grew uneasy; with limited resources and little influence over mainstream space agencies, these researchers could do little more than log their findings and issue quiet alerts to a handful of colleagues.

By the time Venus blazed unnaturally large in the telescopes of backyard observers, and especially those who had been tracking its orbital drift already knew that Venus was no longer where it was supposed to be. And that meant something was very, very wrong!

Chapter 2
Ripples of Understanding

Image: iStock

The Impossible Calculations

Three days had passed since Dr. James Chen last stepped outside the Harvard-Smithsonian Centre for Astrophysics. The mountain of empty coffee cups on his desk told that story plainly enough. His bloodshot eyes struggled to focus, the ghostly outline of his computer screen hovering in his vision even when he looked away. But he couldn't tear himself from what the numbers revealed—a truth so profound that his mind refused to accept it, despite running the calculations dozens of times.

"James, your body needs rest," Dr. Sarah Williams said softly, setting down a steaming cup beside his trembling hands. He glanced up at her—the familiar face of fifteen years' partnership now marked by the same obsession that gripped him. Her lab coat, normally pressed to perfection, hung wrinkled from her shoulders. Her fingers repeatedly raked through her tangled hair, a gesture he recognized as her response to profound anxiety.

"Rest?" James whispered, his voice hoarse from disuse. He turned the screen toward her, his hand shaking slightly. "How can anyone rest after seeing this, Sarah? Look at these numbers. Look at what they're telling us about everything we thought we knew."

The data showed something impossible: Venus was accelerating inward, its orbit degrading in a pattern that defied every model of celestial mechanics they'd ever created. It wasn't just a slight deviation—it was as if someone or something had reached into the solar system and given the planet a push!

Racing Against Time

Sarah pulled up a chair, her own exhaustion evident in the dark circles under her eyes. "Have you seen the latest data from Mauna Kea?"

He nodded grimly. "It confirms everything we're seeing. The question is: How do we tell people?"

That was the crux of it. How do you tell the world that a planet—one they could see with their naked eyes—was behaving impossibly? Already, social media was buzzing with theories. #VenusWatch was trending globally, with everything from legitimate scientific speculation to wild conspiracy theories about alien intervention.

In the conference room down the hall, a team of graduate students was coordinating with observatories worldwide. The walls were covered with printouts—orbital calculations, spectroscopic analyses, gravitational models. Young faces looked increasingly worried as each new piece of data confirmed their worst fears.

"Dr. Chen!" One of the students burst into his office, tablet in hand. "The European Southern Observatory just sent new measurements. The acceleration is increasing!"

James grabbed the tablet, Sarah leaning in close to see. The numbers were clear—Venus wasn't just moving; it was moving faster with each passing day.

The scientific community was struggling to maintain order in their ranks. Emergency conferences were being held virtually around the clock. Theoretical physicists argued with planetary scientists about possible mechanisms. Solar physicists suggested unusual coronal mass ejections might be responsible, while others proposed more exotic explanations involving dark matter or unknown gravitational effects.

"We need to call an emergency meeting," Sarah said, already reaching for her phone. "All departments, all specialties. We need to pool our knowledge."

When Science Meets Uncertainty

Within hours, the main conference room was packed. Astronomers, physicists, geologists, and atmospheric scientists crowded around tables and peered at screens. The air was thick with tension, and too many people were breathing the same recycled air.

"What about gravitational influences from outside the solar system?" suggested Dr. Rodriguez, a visiting researcher from Chile.

"We've checked," James responded, pulling up a star chart. "Nothing massive enough to cause this kind of effect. Besides, it would be affecting other planets too."

"Could it be something internal to Venus?" asked a young postdoc. "Some kind of core dynamics we don't understand?"

The discussions continued late into the night. Theories were proposed and discarded. Mathematical models were built and torn apart. Through it all, the data continued to stream in, each new measurement confirming their growing fears.

In the cafeteria at midnight, James and Sarah sat with cooling cups of vending machine coffee, watching a late-night news report on the wall-mounted TV. The anchor was trying to maintain a calm demeanor while reporting on the growing public interest in Venus's unusual behavior.

"We have to make an announcement," Sarah said quietly. "A real one, not just these vague statements about 'unusual astronomical phenomena.'"

James nodded slowly. "The public deserves to know. But we need to be careful about how we present this. The last thing we need is panic."

As if on cue, his phone buzzed with a message from NASA headquarters. They weren't the only ones reaching this conclusion. A coordinated public announcement was being planned.

The next morning, still without sleep, James found himself in front of a camera, trying to explain the inexplicable to the world. Sarah stood just off-camera, offering silent support as he carefully described what they knew—and what they didn't.

"Venus is exhibiting unprecedented changes in its orbital trajectory," he said, keeping his voice steady. "The scientific community is working around the clock to understand the cause and implications of these changes."

What he didn't say—and couldn't say yet—was that they were terrified! Not just of what was happening to Venus, but of what it meant for their understanding of the universe. If a planet could simply change its orbit, what other assumptions about cosmic stability might be wrong?

As the days passed and Venus grew brighter in the sky, the weight of uncertainty pressed down on them all. Science had always been about pushing the boundaries of knowledge, but now those boundaries were pushing back, revealing how little they truly understood about the cosmic dance they'd thought they knew so well.

Chapter 3
The Fiery Sister

Image: IStock

A Global Scientific Summit

The dying light of day painted Dubai's jagged skyline in hues of amber and gold as Dr. Aisha Hassan stood motionless at her window. Soon, Venus would emerge against the darkening canvas of night, unnaturally brilliant—a familiar celestial neighbour suddenly transformed into something unrecognizable. She pressed her palm against the cool glass, a lifetime of studying Earth's sister planet somehow insufficient for this moment when all her knowledge felt inadequate.

Tomorrow she would face the world's leaders, their expectant eyes fixed on her for answers. Her presentation waited, meticulously prepared with charts and figures and projections, but how could sterile data possibly convey the earth-shattering significance of what they'd discovered? How could she find words to explain that the fundamental principles governing planetary behaviour—principles humanity had built its understanding of the cosmos upon—might crumble under this new evidence?

"Dr. Hassan?" The gentle voice of her assistant Zara broke through her thoughts. "They're gathering for the preliminary briefing."

Aisha drew a deep breath and adjusted her hijab with practiced hands, finding comfort in the familiar gesture before turning to face the wall of screens illuminating her office. One by one, faces materialized—brilliant minds from NASA, ESA, Roscosmos, ISRO, and countless other agencies across the globe. She saw the same haunted look in their eyes that she felt in her soul. These scientists, once divided by national pride and competitive funding, now bound together by circumstances none of them could have imagined—the universe itself defying their collective understanding.

Earth's Turbulent Twin

"Venus was never the serene goddess we named her for," she began, sharing her screen. "She's always been Earth's tempestuous sister, a world of extremes that could have been our twin but took a different path."

The data flowed across their screens—surface temperatures hot enough to melt lead, atmospheric pressure ninety times that of Earth, clouds of sulfuric acid swirling above vast plains of volcanic rock. A world that had long fascinated and frightened scientists in equal measure.

"But now," she continued, pulling up the latest orbital calculations, "something has changed. The planet is moving in ways we can't explain. And we need to understand why."

Her words lingered between them all, suspended like smoke from a lit fuse that no one dared to extinguish. Across the digital divide, Aisha watched the faces of her colleagues—brilliant minds who had charted the stars and unravelled cosmic mysteries for decades—as they exchanged glances heavy with unspoken dread. This wasn't merely an unexpected reading or a curious anomaly. It was something that defied the very foundation of what they understood about our solar system.

The questions came in a rush then, voices overlapping in their urgency, hands gesturing with the nervous energy of those confronting the unknown:

"Could Venus's hellish environment somehow be connected to what we're witnessing?" asked the NASA director, leaning forward until his face dominated his screen.

"Is it possible something has fundamentally altered within its core?" The Indian physicist's voice trembled slightly, betraying the calm she attempted to project.

"Might this be some natural cycle we've simply never documented before?" suggested the Russian astronomer, his weathered face lined with both hope and doubt.

Aisha drew a slow breath into her lungs, feeling the weight of this moment settle across her shoulders. Here was that sacred threshold where human knowledge met the vast expanse of what remained unknown—where certainty dissolved into possibility.

"The truth," she said softly, her voice steady despite the tremor in her heart, "is that we simply don't know. We have theories, hypotheses, educated guesses... but none of us can fully explain what we're witnessing."

In the silence that followed, no one spoke or moved. It was a profound stillness, pregnant with intellectual tension and the collective recognition that they stood at the edge of a paradigm shift. This was the breathless moment before certainty crumbled, before textbooks would need rewriting, before everything they thought they understood about planetary physics would be questioned—the calm before imagination and speculation would flood through the breach in their understanding.

A senior scientist from ESA leaned forward. "Venus has been geologically active in the past, but no model suggests it could suddenly shift its orbit. Could we be seeing the first evidence of a deep internal event, something triggering a shift in the planet's density or momentum?"

Aisha tapped a few keys, pulling up a rotating model of Venus's internal composition. "Venus's core is still largely a mystery to us. It's thought to be at least partially liquid, but if there was some kind of rapid phase transition—say, a sudden redistribution of mass—then we could be looking at an effect we've never accounted for."

A NASA planetary physicist frowned. "If it were an internal process, wouldn't we have seen precursor signs? Thermal anomalies, increased outgassing, or surface deformations?"

"Not necessarily," Aisha said. "Venus's thick atmosphere and its runaway greenhouse effect act like an insulating barrier. Even if a deep subsurface event had been unfolding for years—even centuries—it might not be detectable from the surface."

She paused, then zoomed in on a recent heat map. "However, we have seen sporadic signs of geological activity—thermal emissions near Idunn Mons, trace detections of sulfur dioxide bursts, fluctuations in the cloud deck structure. What if these weren't isolated incidents, but part of a larger systemic shift?"

The murmuring on the call grew louder.

A researcher from Japan cleared his throat. "Could this be linked to solar activity? A previously unknown type of electromagnetic disturbance from the Sun interacting with Venus's atmosphere?"

A scientist from India nodded. "We've seen that Venus's upper atmosphere behaves chaotically—hurricane-force winds, ionospheric disruptions. If an extreme solar event caused some kind of ionospheric instability, could it have affected the planet's overall momentum?"

Aisha frowned. "If that's the case, we'd need to cross-reference with recent solar storms. But it still doesn't explain an orbital shift of this magnitude. The Sun's influence is powerful, but planetary orbits don't just change due to atmospheric turbulence."

Another voice broke in—Dr. Dmitri Volkov from Roscosmos. "Or something external? A gravitational anomaly? A rogue asteroid interaction we haven't accounted for?"

"Unlikely," Aisha countered. "Venus's mass is enormous. Even an asteroid impact—unless it was the size of Ceres or Pluto—wouldn't be enough to alter its orbit this significantly. And if something that large had come close to Venus, we'd have seen disturbances in Mercury's orbit as well."

She hesitated. "And yet…"

Aisha exhaled slowly, her fingers hovering over the keyboard. They couldn't rule anything out.

They were grasping at ideas, pulling theories from the edges of astrophysics. Yet none fit perfectly.

Venus was behaving in a way that defied known science.

Around the world, scientists began reexamining everything they thought they knew about Venus. Supercomputers ran endless simulations, analyzing decades of data collected by the Soviet Venera probes, NASA's Magellan orbiter, and the European Venus Express. Every scrap of information, every pressure reading, every chemical analysis, every radar scan of the planet's surface—became precious.

New deep-learning algorithms were trained overnight, searching for anomalies in historical data that had been overlooked. Scientists combed through old mission archives, scrutinizing telemetry signals, hunting for any sign that Venus had been changing beneath their noses long before they noticed. Had there been signs? Had humanity simply failed to recognize them?

Astronomers rushed to adjust their telescopes. The James Webb Space Telescope, designed for deep-space observations, was now being partially redirected toward Venus. Its infrared instruments scanned the planet's thick sulfuric clouds, measuring thermal emissions with unprecedented accuracy.

The World Mobilisers

On Earth, ground-based observatories in Chile, South Africa, and Hawaii synchronized their efforts, conducting a massive, coordinated sky survey. Observers tracked Venus with laser range-finding, measuring its exact position down to the millimeter. Every deviation, no matter how slight, was logged and analyzed.

A new space race had begun—not to land on another world, but to understand why one was changing before their eyes.

Governments were scrambling. In Washington, national security advisors met behind closed doors, their faces grim. The Pentagon wanted to know if Venus's motion could be weaponized—if a planetary shift of this scale meant something more than a natural event.

The Kremlin issued vague but urgent statements about the need for "international scientific cooperation." Behind the scenes, Russian astrophysicists were in emergency meetings, analyzing Venus's trajectory with a mixture of awe and concern. Could it affect Earth's own gravitational stability?

China announced that its lunar and Mars programs were being temporarily deprioritized. All available resources were being redirected to Venus's research. The Chinese Space Agency ordered immediate modifications to its next-generation probes, repurposing them for Venusian observation rather than deep-space exploration.

In Geneva, the United Nations convened an emergency assembly, bringing together planetary scientists, diplomats, and world leaders.

A single question hung over the session, stark in its simplicity—and its terrifying implications.

What happens if Venus keeps moving?

Later that night, Aisha sat with Zara, reviewing their presentation for world leaders. They had stripped away the technical jargon and focused on the essential facts. But how do you explain to politicians that a planet has gone rogue?

"Do you think they'll understand the implications?" Zara asked, making notes on her tablet.

"They'll have to," Aisha replied. "Because whatever's happening to Venus, we need to prepare for the possibilities."

Zara hesitated before speaking again. "And what if the possibility is... worst-case scenario?"

Aisha exhaled, pressing her fingers against her temples. The worst-case scenario. She had run the numbers. If Venus's trajectory continued to shift toward Earth—even by the slightest margin—it would eventually disrupt gravitational balances across the solar system. Tidal forces would intensify. The Moon's orbit could be affected. And if Venus came too close, Earth's own atmosphere could change in ways they hadn't even begun to model.

A Mirror to Earth's Future

But there was another possibility, one even more terrifying in its implications.

Venus was proof that a planet could become inhospitable. Its runaway greenhouse effect had turned it into a searing wasteland. It wasn't always this way—scientists believed that billions of years ago, Venus had water, possibly oceans.

If Earth's climate followed the same path, if CO_2 levels continued to rise unchecked, could humanity someday look up at Venus and see its own future reflected back?

The connection was impossible to ignore.

Aisha added a final slide to her presentation.

"Venus: A Planetary Mirror?"

The next morning, facing the assembled leaders on her screen, Aisha felt the weight of history. Their decisions in the coming weeks would shape humanity's response to an unprecedented crisis.

"Venus is our closest planetary neighbor," she explained. "What affects her may ultimately affect us. We need to act now, while we still have time to study and understand these changes."

For a long moment, silence filled the virtual conference room. Then a voice—calm but firm—spoke from the screen. It was the representative from China.

"What do you need from us?"

Aisha straightened. "Satellite coordination, atmospheric monitoring, and immediate resource allocation to observatories worldwide. If Venus is giving us a warning, we need to listen."

In homes, schools, and offices around the world, people looked up at the brightening evening star with new eyes.

Venus had always been there, constant in mythology, history, and science.

Now, it was something else.

A mystery. A threat. A warning.

And beyond Aisha's office window, the evening star continued to shine—brilliant, unyielding, whispering secrets humanity had only begun to understand.

Chapter 4
Gathering Storm

Image: iStock

The First Signs of Panic

The first major signs of panic appeared three weeks after the initial discovery. Despite efforts to maintain calm—despite careful statements from space agencies and governments—fear began to spread like a virus through the connected world.

Venus had changed. And no one knew what it meant.

Dr. Angela Martinez stood by her apartment window in Manhattan, watching the chaos unfold below. The city had always pulsed with a predictable rhythm—morning commutes, lunchtime crowds, weekend markets—but now, something fundamental had changed. The usual flow of life had been disrupted, replaced by an uneasy energy that crackled through the streets like static before a storm.

People gathered in clusters, their faces turned skyward, staring at Venus as it burned brightly in the evening sky. There was a feverish quality to their movements, an urgency that had not been there weeks ago. Some carried hastily made signs, their bold, frantic handwriting scrawled across cardboard and bedsheets. One read "THE SKY IS FALLING!" in thick black paint, the letters smudged as if the writer's hands had been shaking. Another declared "VENUS IS A WARNING—REPENT!" while a third, held high by a pale, wide-eyed woman, simply stated "THE GODS ARE ANGRY."

Others stood in silent awe, their gazes locked onto the once-familiar planet that had become an unsettling presence in the heavens. Some wept quietly. Some whispered prayers. A few clutched rosaries, worry beads, or other symbols of faith. Others held nothing at all, just staring, frozen, as if waiting for the sky to crack open.

Angela reached for her phone and opened her research notes, recording an entry with slow, deliberate speech. The file was titled "Social Response to Astronomical Anomaly: Initial Observations."

"The fascinating thing," she dictated, "is how quickly traditional social boundaries break down in the face of cosmic uncertainty. People who normally wouldn't interact—neighbors who ignored each other, strangers who shared nothing in common—are forming spontaneous communities, sharing theories and fears. A primal instinct emerges, one that transcends nationality, class, or belief systems. The idea that the universe may not be as stable as we believed is unearthing something ancient in us all."

Her phone buzzed—a new message from Dr. Dmitri Volkov in Moscow. Their collaboration had begun almost accidentally, sparked by a late-night academic exchange, but now they were leading a global study on human responses to the Venus phenomenon.

"Public reaction varies by culture," his message read, "but underlying patterns are consistent. People seek community, answers, and purpose. The desire to impose meaning on uncertainty is universal."

A World Transformed by Fear

Angela glanced back outside. The crowd had doubled, spilling into adjacent streets. Someone had set up a makeshift telescope, the kind usually reserved for summer stargazing events in Central Park. Despite the overwhelming light pollution of the city, a line had already formed.

Some were families with children, parents lifting them onto their shoulders so they could peer through the lens, their young voices filled with curiosity and unease. Others were elderly couples, standing quietly together, holding hands as they waited for their turn. A man in a business suit—tie loosened, face drawn—stood near a teenage girl in a hoodie, neither speaking, both watching the sky.

Angela pressed her forehead against the glass. They were desperate to see it with their own eyes.

It wasn't enough to read the news, to watch the broadcasts, to listen to scientists explain the data. They needed to look at Venus themselves, to confirm that it was real, to absorb the sheer impossibility of what was unfolding.

Angela's fingers tightened around her phone. The world was watching, but no one knew what they were waiting for.

When Science Meets Spirituality

In Paris, the steps of Notre Dame Cathedral flickered with the glow of thousands of candles. People knelt together, whispering prayers beneath the towering gothic spires. Some recited ancient hymns, voices trembling with reverence and fear. Others sat in silence, their faces turned toward the night sky, where Venus burned brighter than it ever had before. A priest spoke softly to a weeping woman, her hands clasped so tightly that her knuckles had turned white. "We must not see this as a curse," he said. "Perhaps it is a lesson, a reminder of our place in the universe."

In New Delhi, temple bells rang deep into the night, the sound rippling across the city like a heartbeat. Priests gathered in circles, engaged in fervent debate. Was Venus's movement a sign from the gods? A celestial realignment meant to restore balance? Or was it something darker, a warning of imminent cosmic upheaval? Worshippers came in droves, pressing their palms together in silent prayer as they stared at the sky, waiting for an answer that no scripture could provide.

In Cape Town, radio stations became battlegrounds for scientists and religious leaders, their discussions oscillating between rational inquiry and existential dread. A well-known astrophysicist insisted on air that Venus's motion was explainable, that science would provide an answer.

A theologian countered, asking if humanity's arrogance had blinded them to a greater truth. "Perhaps," he said, his voice grave, "this is not an error in our calculations but a revelation we were never meant to understand."

In Tokyo, neon billboards lit up the skyline, no longer displaying advertisements for cars and cosmetics, but instead streaming real-time Venus data. Temperature readings. Velocity updates. AI-generated hypothetical futures. Some screens projected scientific models, illustrating possible orbital shifts. Others leaned into fear, flashing apocalyptic imagery—Venus colliding with Earth, tsunamis swallowing cities, a planet consumed in flames. Beneath the artificial glow of the screens, people moved quietly, tensely, as if afraid to break the fragile illusion of normalcy.

In Sydney, Australians gathered on the beaches, building "end-of-the-world" bonfires. The air was thick with the scent of salt and burning wood. Some laughed, drinking and singing as though daring the universe to prove them wrong. Others sat alone, toes buried in the sand, staring at the sky with tears glistening in the firelight. For many, this was not just a night of celebration or fear. It was a reckoning.

Angela's eyes burned as she scrolled through her news feed, witnessing humanity's collective response unfold in real time. The Vatican had released a measured statement calling for cooperation between faith and scientific inquiry—a bridge across troubled waters. Meanwhile, in the humid heart of Brazil, an obscure cult gathered beneath the stars, declaring Venus an unmistakable harbinger of divine judgment, their whispered warnings of apocalypse spreading like wildfire. In Texas, a televangelist's voice thundered through a massive amphitheatre, his words reverberating through thousands of raised hands and upturned faces: "This," he proclaimed, his voice cracking with emotion, "is the first trumpet of Revelation!" The answering roar from the congregation seemed to shake the very foundations of the building, a primal expression of both terror and validation.

Faith, Fear and Public Reactions

The digital realm amplified these reactions a thousandfold. **#VenusSignal** dominated every platform, a kaleidoscope of human reaction ranging from reasoned speculation to unbridled panic. Some messages screamed in all-caps urgency: "THE GOVERNMENT KNEW ALL ALONG!" Others wove elaborate narratives of alien contact and tears in the fabric of reality. One theory—shared hundreds of thousands of times despite its absurdity—insisted that Venus had somehow been replaced by a disguised black hole, its unnatural brightness merely the final light show before Earth's inevitable consumption.

Angela closed her burning eyes, pressing cool fingertips against her throbbing temples. She could feel it happening—the dissolving boundary between verifiable fact and contagious fear, the collective sanity of the world unravelling thread by thread before her.

Half a world away, Dmitri Volkov hunched in his Moscow office, the harsh blue light from his monitor carving deep shadows across his unshaven face. The tea beside him had long since surrendered its warmth to the night air, forgotten in the face of what he was seeing. His eyes never left the NASA and ESA simulations streaming in, each new dataset more impossible to rationalize than the last. Venus wasn't simply moving—it was accelerating.

His fingers hovered above his keyboard, trembling slightly before he composed his message to Angela: "We need to prepare people." A heartbeat of hesitation, then: "The psychological impact of what's coming..." The sentence remained unfinished, the implications too overwhelming to articulate.

Angela understood without explanation. Her research had already mapped the emotional journey unfolding across humanity. First came denial—the reflexive rejection of an unthinkable truth. Then panic, a desperate scramble for answers amid growing suspicion of those who claimed to know them. Obsession followed, with theories multiplying as people combed through ancient texts and questioned whether Venus had ever truly been the planet they believed it to be. And finally, the great divide: resignation or action—some surrendering to paralysing fear while others searched frantically for any path forward through this unprecedented moment.

The austere lecture halls of Stockholm University—once the domain of scattered students and academic rigor—now overflowed with humanity. People sat shoulder to shoulder in the aisles, stood pressed against walls, and crowded doorways, drawn to philosophers whose words had previously echoed through half-empty rooms. These thinkers, with their weathered books and decades of contemplating existence on society's intellectual fringes, found themselves thrust into an unexpected spotlight.

Gray-haired professors who had spent lifetimes exploring the terrain of human meaning now faced seas of anxious faces—bankers, nurses, construction workers, grandmothers—all united in their sudden, visceral need to make sense of a cosmos that had betrayed their understanding. Their lectures on human fragility against the vastness of an indifferent universe no longer felt like abstract intellectual exercises but an urgent cartography for navigating this new reality.

As night fell and Venus blazed its impossible path across the sky, people lingered after these talks, forming tight circles of conversation, strangers becoming confidants through shared existential trembling. They clung to phrases from the lecturers—"cosmic insignificance" and "authentic existence"—as if these concepts might form handrails along the precipice of uncertainty. The philosophers themselves seemed transformed, their lifetime of theoretical preparation suddenly practical, their eyes reflecting both the weight of responsibility and a strange vindication.

"What does it mean to be human," asked one silver-haired woman, her voice carrying through a packed hall, "when we discover that the universe itself refuses to follow the laws we believed governed it?" In the silence that followed, two hundred strangers breathed as one organism, united not by answers, but by the profound recognition of the question that had kept them all staring at their ceilings through sleepless nights.

Society's Fragile Balance

Governments scrambled. Some assured the public there was nothing to fear, urging trust in science. Others activated classified contingency plans, shifting military satellites from Earth surveillance to Venus's tracking. Billionaires fled to private islands, as if a celestial catastrophe could be outrun. The United Nations formed an emergency coalition—not just to understand Venus, but to manage Earth's unraveling reaction to it.

The financial markets trembled, uncertainty rippling through every sector. Traders watched in stunned silence as stocks plummeted, long-term investments abandoned in favor of immediate survival strategies. Insurance companies faced an unprecedented flood of "Act of God" claims, policyholders desperate to secure payouts for disasters that had not yet come. Gold prices soared, becoming the last refuge of those who believed in tangible security. Survival gear vanished from shelves, as demand outpaced supply.

In some places, fear mutated into violence. In Jakarta and São Paulo, riots erupted, fueled by misinformation and desperation. Streets burned as protestors clashed with authorities, some demanding answers, others seeking scapegoats. In Montana, survivalist communities fortified their compounds, stockpiling weapons and rations, convinced that Venus was a cover-up for an impending government collapse.

In Berlin, a cyber-attack plunged sections of the city into darkness. Anarchist groups claimed responsibility, insisting that Venus was not a cosmic mystery, but an engineered crisis, a tool of control to enslave humanity.

Yet not all responses were irrational. In laboratories, research centers, and think tanks, minds sharpened under pressure. If Venus had rewritten the rules of the cosmos, then humanity would have to adapt, or be left behind.

For the first time in history, borders meant nothing. Scientists, once divided by politics and competition, worked together as if the fate of humanity depended on it—because, in a way, it did. Data flowed freely between nations; theories revised in real time as the brightest minds on Earth chased an answer to the unanswerable.

Beyond the laboratories, the world found its own ways to cope. Musicians wrote songs about Venus, melodies tinged with both fear and wonder. Their voices carried across radios, filling the air with haunting ballads about a sky - transformed. In the streets, artists painted Venus into murals, capturing its eerie glow in strokes of crimson and gold. Walls once covered in advertisements and graffiti now told the story of a planet reborn in fire and mystery.

Children sent letters to NASA, their innocent questions cut through the chaos. Some asked if Venus would hurt them. Others, with hope in their hearts, wanted to know: "Can we save Venus?"

Angela documented it all, knowing this moment would define human history. Would humanity unite under the weight of the unknown, or would it break apart?

Outside, Venus burned brighter, and the world held its breath. No one knew what would happen when it finally exhaled.

Chapter 5
The Last Hope Initiative

Venus Impacting Earth

Image: iStock

Sarah Chen hadn't seen her family in three weeks. The NASA command center had become her home, its fluorescent lights and endless screens her constant companions. She sat now, coffee gone cold beside her keyboard, watching as another simulation failed. The bags under her eyes told a story of countless nights spent searching for solutions, each one more desperate than the last.

"We have to try something else," she murmured, more to herself than to her colleagues scattered around the room. The space felt smaller these days, despite half the staff working remotely. Perhaps it was the weight of responsibility that made the walls feel closer, the air heavier.

Across the globe, humanity was pulling together in ways previously unimaginable. The old borders and rivalries that had defined

35

international relations for centuries seemed to melt away in the face of Venus's approach. Russian rocket scientists collaborated with their American counterparts over video calls that stretched into the night. Chinese supercomputers ran simulations developed by European teams. The International Space Station had become a command hub, its crew doubled as they coordinated the most ambitious space mission in human history.

Yet for all their combined brilliance, for all the resources suddenly made available when governments realized money would mean nothing if Earth itself was destroyed, they kept hitting the same wall: Venus was simply too massive.

"What about the Hail Mary project?" Dr. Yamamoto asked from his station near the main display. The project was their last, best hope— a constellation of nuclear devices that might, theoretically, alter Venus's trajectory just enough to avoid catastrophe. The chances of success were microscopic, but they were better than nothing.

Sarah pulled up the latest calculations. "We'd need every launch vehicle on Earth, working in perfect coordination. And even then..." She let the sentence hang unfinished. They all knew the odds.

Standing Together

Outside the scientific community, humanity faced the crisis in countless different ways. In Nebraska, farmers planted their fields despite knowing they might never see the harvest—an act of defiance against cosmic indifference. In Vatican City, the Pope led prayers that united billions across faiths, the shared language of hope transcending traditional boundaries. In a small apartment in Tokyo, a young couple decided to have their baby anyway, choosing to believe in tomorrow.

Underground cities were taking shape, though everyone knew they could only save a fraction of the population. The Svalbard Global Seed Vault expanded its capacity, preserving the genetic heritage of Earth's plant life. Libraries digitized their collections at unprecedented rates, uploading humanity's accumulated knowledge to hardened servers and space-based data centers.

The darkness in human nature revealed itself too amid the crisis—streets erupted in violence, opportunists exploited fear for profit, and some abandoned themselves to pleasure's embrace, believing tomorrow might never arrive. In certain cities, the fragile structure of society began to fracture beneath the weight of cosmic uncertainty. Yet even as chaos bloomed, so too did extraordinary compassion—people opening their homes to those they'd never met, neighbourhoods forming impromptu communities of mutual support, strangers risking their safety to protect one another.

Sarah contemplated this complex tapestry of human response as her eyes burned from staring at her monitor, running yet another simulation through the night. Her phone buzzed regularly with messages from her parents, pleading with increasing desperation for her to abandon her work and return home—to spend whatever precious days remained surrounded by those who loved her. But she couldn't tear herself away. Not while even the faintest possibility remained.

The soft electronic ping cut through her exhaustion. New data arriving from the European Space Agency. She opened the file automatically, expecting merely another confirmation of their collective doom. Instead, her breath caught in her throat as the numbers revealed something unexpected.

"Dr. Yamamoto," she called across the lab, her voice betraying none of the wild hope suddenly pounding through her veins. "These gravitational calculations... you need to see this."

The older scientist wheeled his chair to her station, the dark circles beneath his eyes testament to weeks without proper rest. He leaned forward, scanning the data with practiced precision until understanding dawned across his features.

"If we time it perfectly," Sarah whispered, afraid to give full voice to hope, "and I mean with absolute precision, we might leverage Earth's own gravitational field. Not to halt Venus, but to..."

Humanity's Finest Hour

"To guide it," he finished, wonder creeping into his voice. "Into a new orbital pattern altogether."

Something long absent filled the fluorescent-lit room—a flicker of genuine possibility warming the cold space of despair. It wasn't certainty—they were galaxies away from that. But it was a chance where before there had been none. And throughout human history, a single chance had often been the seedbed of miracles.

Sarah's fingers flew across her keyboard, calculating the exact parameters they would need, the precise moment when intervention might alter destiny. Her eyes briefly drifted to the photograph taped to her monitor—her five-year-old niece gazing upward at a night sky, her expression one of innocent wonder rather than terror. This, Sarah realized with sudden clarity, was the true heart of their struggle. Not merely survival but preserving a world where children could still look skyward with awe rather than dread.

The laboratory hummed with renewed purpose as team members reached out to colleagues across the globe, time zones and national borders rendered meaningless by shared necessity. Outside, Venus gleamed brilliantly in the deepening twilight—transformed in their perception from harbinger of extinction to perhaps something more profound: a cosmic examination of humanity's capacity for resilience, innovation, and above all, unity in the face of universal challenge.

They were, after all, more than just individuals or nations now. They were Earth's children, standing together at a crossroads of history. And perhaps that unity, that shared purpose, was itself a kind of victory, regardless of what the coming months might bring.

Sarah's discovery offered hope, but time was brutally short. As teams worldwide coordinated the unprecedented effort to influence Venus's trajectory, the planet's presence in Earth's sky grew more ominous with each passing day. Amateur astronomers reported that Venus now appeared nearly twice its normal size, its brilliant light casting distinct shadows even in urban areas.

In New York, the streets had largely emptied. Those who remained witnessed an eerie twilight at noon as Venus's gravitational influence began distorting Earth's atmosphere. The oceans responded too - tidal patterns shifted dramatically, forcing coastal evacuations worldwide. In Japan, fishing fleets sat idle in their harbors, their crews unwilling to venture into increasingly unpredictable waters.

Dr. Yamamoto's family had begged him to join them in their designated shelter, but like Sarah, he couldn't leave. His youngest daughter had pressed her favorite lucky charm into his hand before departing - it now sat next to his computer, a small plastic cat with one paw raised in greeting.

"Final simulation running," Sarah announced, her voice steady despite her trembling hands. The room fell silent except for the hum of overworked computers. Outside, the sky had taken on an unsettling purple hue, a visual reminder of the physics they were attempting to harness.

Governments had positioned their nuclear arsenals, converting weapons of war into humanity's last hope for survival. The plan required synchronization down to the millisecond - even a slight delay could mean the difference between deflection and devastation. Every space agency on Earth had linked their systems, creating a unified network that would either save humanity or witness its end.

"If this doesn't work," Dr. Yamamoto said quietly, "I want you to know-"

"Don't," Sarah cut him off. "We're not doing goodbyes. Not yet."

The simulation completed with a soft chime. Sarah stared at the results, double-checking every variable, every calculation. After what felt like eternity, she looked up at her colleagues, her eyes bright with unshed tears.

"It's time," she said simply.

Around the world, billions huddled in shelters, watching screens or hugging loved ones. Some prayed, some sang, some simply waited in silence. In orbit, astronauts on the International Space Station prepared to witness either humanity's greatest achievement or its final moments.

Sarah's fingers hovered over the keyboard, her breath shallow. The numbers on the screen blurred in her vision as exhaustion pressed against her skull. She blinked hard and forced herself to focus. The simulation had finished running, but the result was the same— Venus's trajectory still led toward Earth.

The tension in the room was suffocating.

The Hail Mary Plan

Dr. Yamamoto, standing beside her, adjusted his glasses and exhaled sharply. "The window is closing. If we don't act within the next twenty-four hours, we lose any chance of intervention."

Sarah's throat tightened. The plan—their last, desperate attempt to shift Venus's orbit—depended on an almost impossibly precise series of detonations and gravitational nudges. And even then, it was more of a prayer than a calculation.

"Run it again," she said.

One of the technicians hesitated. "Dr. Chen, we've already—"

"Run. It. Again."

The room hummed as the simulation restarted. Sarah's eyes flicked to the wall monitors displaying the latest images of Venus. It was now so bright in the night sky that even city dwellers could see it clearly. Reports were flooding in from across the globe—coastal waters swelling unpredictably, tides behaving erratically. The gravitational pull was already being felt.

How much worse would it get?

Across the room, another monitor flickered with live footage from cities worldwide. Some streets were eerily empty, people sheltering in place. Others were full of makeshift celebrations, weddings, vigils, final goodbyes. In some places, violence had erupted as fear overtook reason. Humanity was bracing for either salvation or destruction, with no middle ground left to stand on.

Sarah turned back to her screen. The simulation reached its final stage. The result was populated.

Her pulse stilled.

"Wait," she whispered. She ran the numbers again, fingers flying across the keys. She checked the gravitational calculations, cross-referencing them against real-time data from the European Southern Observatory. The air in the room grew electric, as others leaned in.

Dr. Yamamoto caught it first. "It's slowing."

Sarah nodded, hardly daring to believe it. "The acceleration—it's decreasing."

The whisper spread through the command center like wildfire. Scientists murmured, hands clapping over mouths, eyes flicking between screens.

"How is that possible?" someone asked.

Sarah didn't have an answer. But she had a theory.

"What if—what if the gravitational assist from Earth isn't just affecting Venus? What if Venus is influencing itself?" Her hands trembled as she sketched out an orbital map, adjusting for the latest velocity readings. "If we nudge it at precisely the right moment, we might not need the full detonation sequence."

Dr. Yamamoto caught on immediately. "You're saying it's naturally finding a resonance point?"

"A new equilibrium," she whispered.

For the first time in weeks, hope didn't feel like a lie.

Chapter 6
A New Equilibrium

Image: NASA

A computer-enhanced image of the surface of Venus.

The Moment the World Held Its Breath

For a moment, there was nothing.

The silence was deafening, stretching impossibly long, as if the universe itself was holding its breath. Humanity had spent weeks preparing for impact, for catastrophe, for the violent reshaping of the solar system itself. But now—now something else was happening.

Venus was slowing.

Sarah stood motionless; eyes locked onto the shifting orbital projections. Around her, the command center remained eerily quiet, as if no one dared to believe what they were seeing. Screens flickered with updated calculations, each confirming the impossible. Scientists across the globe scrambled to verify the data, their voices hushed with disbelief.

"How is this even possible?" someone whispered.

Dr. Yamamoto inhaled sharply. "It shouldn't be," he murmured. "But it is."

The atmosphere in the room shifted from dread to cautious hope. Venus, the celestial intruder they had feared for so long, was no longer hurtling toward Earth with devastating certainty. Instead, its trajectory had begun to stabilize—subtly, miraculously—into an orbital resonance that no one had predicted.

News stations across the world struggled to keep up with the changing reality. Live broadcasts that had been preparing to report on an impending catastrophe suddenly found themselves narrating a cosmic mystery. Fear still lingered in every voice, but now it was laced with something else—wonder, relief, awe. Humanity had survived the impossible.

Sarah exhaled for what felt like the first time in days. She glanced at the photo of her niece taped to her workstation, at the little girl who might now grow up in a world forever changed.

And then Sarah let go!

She stumbled back from her console, hands trembling, the breath she'd held finally bursting out in a choking, half-laughing sob. Yamamoto gripped the edge of the desk, then buried his face in his hands. Across the room, a junior technician yelped—not from fear, but from raw, animal joy. It was a sound that echoed through the corridors like thunder, and it broke the dam.

Cheers. Tears. Collapse. A room of exhausted minds and frightened hearts erupted with the primal force of life refusing to be extinguished.

Outside the building, someone had been filming the sky. When the news broke, they turned the camera toward the streets, where strangers were embracing—crying openly, clinging to each other as though just learning the world hadn't ended after all.

In Vatican City, church bells rang before the Pope even gave the word. In New Delhi, fireworks exploded over temple spires. On the beaches of Australia, people danced barefoot in the surf, singing songs that belonged to no one and everyone.

In Moscow, Dmitri Volkov slumped over his desk, tears streaking down his unshaven face as he whispered, *"We made it."*

In New York, Angela watched the city light up—not from fear this time, but in joy. The headlights that had once fled now flowed back in streams of blinking, honking defiance. Humanity was still here.

For a brief and shining moment, the planet remembered how to breathe as one.

And in the night sky, Venus glowed—not as an omen, but as a mystery once again. Still beautiful. Still terrifying. But now, perhaps… merciful.

Venus had not destroyed Earth. But it had rewritten the sky.

In the seventy-two hours after the first signs of Venus's deceleration, humanity existed in a state of suspended animation. The immediate panic had subsided, replaced by a collective holding of breath. No one yet dared to believe in salvation.

Sarah stood before the wall of monitors in NASA's command centre, her body desperately craving sleep while her mind refused to surrender consciousness. She'd been awake for nearly forty hours straight, surviving on vending machine coffee and the occasional protein bar pressed into her hand by concerned colleagues. The data continued to stream in—each new calculation confirming what still seemed impossible.

Venus was stabilizing.

Tony Carrucan

"You should rest," Dr. Yamamoto said quietly, appearing at her side. The older scientist looked equally exhausted, his usually immaculate appearance now dishevelled, his eyes rimmed with red.

"I can't," Sarah replied, not taking her eyes from the screens. "What if we're wrong? What if it's just temporary?"

"Then we'll deal with it," he said. "But right now, the numbers are consistent. Whatever force altered Venus's trajectory is now allowing it to find equilibrium."

On the main screen, the orbital projection showed Venus's new path— a graceful ellipse that would bring it closer to Earth than it had been for millions of years, but not catastrophically so. The planet would settle into a near-resonant orbit, more like a dance partner than a colliding asteroid.

"We need to be absolutely certain before we tell people," Sarah whispered. The weight of this responsibility felt crushing. After weeks of preparing the world for disaster, how did you pivot to announcing salvation without seeming either foolish or manipulative?

Between Crisis and Relief

In cities across the world, a strange limbo had taken hold. The initial wave of panic had crested and broken, leaving behind a landscape of half-empty streets, makeshift shelters, and wary faces turned skyward.

In central London, families who had packed emergency bags now hesitated by their front doors, unsure whether to flee or stay. Reports were filtering through—conflicting, confusing, cautiously optimistic. Some claimed Venus had stopped its advance. Others insisted it was merely slowing before an inevitable collision.

The Thames Barrier had been raised days ago, a precaution against the predicted tidal surges. Now it stood like a monument to fear itself, casting long shadows over waters that remained, for the moment, calm.

45

In a Parisian square, a group of students who had been holding a continuous vigil for nine days straight huddled around a radio. The official announcement was coming within the hour. They clung to each other, a tangle of unwashed bodies and desperate hope.

"My father says it's all been a mistake," a young woman said, her voice cracking with exhaustion. "That the scientists got it wrong."

"Or perhaps they got it right," an older man replied. He had joined their vigil three days ago, bringing blankets and bread. "Perhaps they helped change its course."

No one responded. The idea that human intervention could alter a planet's trajectory seemed as fantastical as the crisis itself. Yet something had changed. Venus's brilliant glow remained in their sky, but its message had transformed from threat to enigma.

The Official Announcement

In the UN Security Council's emergency chamber, world leaders and scientific advisors gathered in solemn assembly. The tension was palpable, faces strained by weeks of crisis management and minimal sleep.

Dr. Aisha Hassan stood at the podium; her usual composure tested by the magnitude of what she had to convey. Behind her, a series of complex orbital diagrams displayed the latest data.

"With a confidence level of 97.8 percent," she said, her voice steady despite her racing heart, "we can confirm that Venus is no longer on a collision course with Earth."

A murmur rippled through the chamber.

"The planet has begun to stabilize into what appears to be a new orbital pattern—one that will place it approximately 20 million kilometres from Earth at its closest approach. This is substantially closer than its previous orbit but does not pose an immediate threat to our planet."

"How can we be certain this stabilization will continue?" The French representative leaned forward, her expression sceptical. "What guarantee do we have that this isn't merely temporary?"

Dr. Hassan nodded. "A valid concern. We have run over fourteen thousand simulations using data from observatories worldwide. All indicate that Venus is finding a gravitational equilibrium—a resonance with Earth that appears to be self-sustaining."

"And what caused this change in the first place?" The Russian diplomat's voice carried an edge of suspicion. "If we don't understand what moved Venus, how can we trust it won't move again?"

A heavy silence fell over the room. This was the question that haunted every scientist, every leader—the fundamental mystery at the heart of everything.

"We don't know," Dr. Hassan admitted. "And I won't pretend otherwise. What we witnessed defies our current understanding of celestial mechanics. It will take years, perhaps decades, of study to comprehend fully."

The Chinese representative stood slowly. "Then what do we tell our people? That the crisis is over, but we have no explanation? That it might happen again at any moment?"

Dr. Hassan took a deep breath. "We tell them the truth. That Venus has found a new orbit. That immediate danger has passed. And that this event has revealed how much we still have to learn about our solar system." She paused. "Most importantly, we tell them that this gives us an unprecedented opportunity to study Venus up close—to understand more about planetary climate systems, including our own."

The UN Secretary-General moved to the center of the chamber. "We must coordinate our message carefully. Panic can subside as quickly as it arose, but uncertainty and confusion could linger for years."

Around the table, heads nodded in solemn agreement. The crisis may have passed, but the world they would return to had been fundamentally altered. Trust in scientific authority, in governmental competence, in cosmic stability itself—all had been shaken to their core.

For ordinary citizens, the transition from apocalyptic fear to cautious relief came in irregular waves. News of Venus's stabilization spread unevenly, creating a patchwork of reactions across the globe.

In Mexico City's Zócalo, where thousands had gathered in communal prayer over the past weeks, the first announcement was met with scepticism. Too many doomsday predictions had been made and withdrawn over the years. The crowd dispersed slowly, reluctantly, as if their continued vigil might somehow help maintain Venus's new, safer path.

In rural Karnataka, India, villages that had been performing continuous pujas to appease the celestial powers now shifted to ceremonies of gratitude. Elderly women threw marigold petals skyward while explaining to wide-eyed children that the goddess had shown mercy after hearing their devotions.

On social media, hashtags transformed overnight: #VenusDoomsday and #FinalDays gave way to #VenusMiracle and #SecondChance. Conspiracy theories evolved just as quickly, with claims that governments had known all along that Venus would stabilize, or that secret technology had been deployed to "tame" the planet.

Dr. Elena Marchant found herself becoming an unlikely media figure, her clear explanations and unassuming demeanour making her a trusted voice amid the confusion. In a CNN interview that would later be viewed over two billion times, she gently corrected the host's suggestion that the crisis had been overblown.

"Not at all," she said firmly. "Venus did change its orbit dramatically. It is now settling into a new configuration—one that could have profound implications for our understanding of planetary dynamics. What we witnessed wasn't a false alarm; it was a genuine cosmic event unlike anything recorded in human history."

"So we're safe now?" the interviewer pressed

A World Changed Forever

Dr. Marchant smiled slightly. "The immediate threat has passed. But 'safe' is a relative term in astronomy. What this event should teach us is humility—a recognition that the universe still holds many mysteries, and that Earth exists within a dynamic solar system, not a static one."

Three weeks after the first signs of Venus's stabilization, Sarah finally returned to her apartment. The place felt alien, like a museum exhibit of her former life. Mail had piled up beneath the slot. Plants had withered on the windowsill. A half-empty coffee mug still sat on the counter, growing a garden of mould—a relic from the morning when everything changed.

She opened the blinds and looked up at the evening sky. Venus blazed there, brighter than ever before, no longer a harbinger of doom but something else entirely—a celestial question mark, a cosmic neighbour suddenly drawn closer.

Her phone buzzed with a notification. Public astronomical observatories were reopening tomorrow, offering special "Venus Viewing" events. Schools were resuming normal schedules. Airlines were gradually restarting flights that had been grounded during the crisis.

The world was cautiously exhaling, returning to routines while absorbing the knowledge that everything had changed. Venus now permanently occupied a different position in Earth's sky—and in humanity's consciousness.

Sarah's doorbell rang. It was her sister and five-year-old niece, Mei, the first family members she'd seen in over a month.

"Auntie Sarah!" Mei rushed forward, wrapping small arms around Sarah's legs. "Did you save us from the angry planet?"

Sarah laughed, lifting the child up. "The planet was never angry, sweetie. Just... moving. And lots of scientists worked together to understand what was happening."

Her sister embraced her tightly. "The news said your team helped track Venus's new orbit."

"We were just one part of a global effort," Sarah said, the exhaustion suddenly hitting her anew.

Later, as evening deepened, the three of them stood on Sarah's small balcony. Mei pointed excitedly at Venus, now blazing golden in the twilight.

"It's so big!" she exclaimed.

"It's closer than it used to be," Sarah explained. "It's going to be our close companion from now on."

"Is that good or bad?" her sister asked quietly.

Sarah considered the question, watching the planet that had nearly brought apocalypse and was now settling into a new celestial rhythm with Earth.

"I think... it's an opportunity," she said finally. "Venus has stories to tell us—about planetary systems, about climate change, about cosmic evolution. And now it's close enough that we might actually hear them."

Mei yawned, leaning against her mother. "I think the planet just got lonely," she mumbled sleepily. "It wanted to come say hello."

Sarah smiled at the child's simple interpretation. Perhaps there was wisdom there—a recognition that even in the vastness of space, proximity mattered. Venus and Earth, two sisters in the solar system, now locked in a closer dance than ever before.

The transition from crisis to new normal would take time. Trust would need to be rebuilt. Scientific models would need to be rewritten. Religious and philosophical frameworks would need to accommodate the knowledge that the cosmos was more dynamic, more changeable than previously believed.

But as Sarah watched Venus gleaming in the darkening sky, she felt something she hadn't experienced in weeks: hope. Not just relief that destruction had been averted, but genuine hope that this cosmic shake-up might awaken humanity to both its vulnerability and its potential.

Venus had changed its path. Perhaps Earth's inhabitants could change theirs as well.

Embracing the New Cosmic Reality

In the following months, observatories worldwide reported unprecedented public interest. People who had never before given a thought to astronomy now lined up for hours to glimpse Venus through telescopes. Schools adjusted their curricula to include more planetary science. Applications to astrophysics programs soared.

The night sky, once taken for granted as merely a backdrop to human affairs, had reasserted itself in the collective consciousness as an active, dynamic realm—one that could intrude upon terrestrial concerns with little warning.

Gradually, a strange new normal emerged. Weather forecasts began including "Venus visibility ratings" alongside temperature and precipitation. Artists incorporated the planet's enhanced glow into paintings, sculptures, and architectural lighting. Children born after the event would grow up with a different celestial landscape than any previous generation had known, with Venus commanding the heavens as a golden sentinel, nearly twice its former apparent size.

Some psychological effects lingered longer. A wave of "cosmic anxiety" was documented among populations worldwide—a persistent unease about celestial stability, a heightened awareness of Earth's vulnerability in the vastness of space. Therapists developed specialized techniques to address this new form of existential distress.

Yet alongside this anxiety came something else: a renewed sense of Earth as a single, shared habitat. National boundaries had meant nothing in the face of Venus's approach. The planet's changed orbit now served as a constant reminder visible from every continent—a celestial monument to humanity's shared destiny.

Six months after the crisis, an international conference convened to establish the Venus Monitoring Network—a coordinated global effort to observe and study Earth's newly proximate neighbour. For the first time, space agencies that had once competed now pooled resources and data, united by curiosity about the celestial dance unfolding above.

In her journal, Sarah wrote: "We still don't understand what forces moved Venus from its ancient path. Perhaps we never will. But its new proximity has moved us too—shifted our perspective, altered our priorities. We look up more often now. We pay attention. And maybe, just maybe, that's exactly what we needed."

Venus shone down on a changed Earth—and an Earth more aware of cosmic change.

The planet's acceleration continued to slow, its trajectory gradually stabilizing into what astronomers would later call a "resonant orbital configuration" with Earth. Rather than the feared collision, Venus had settled into a new, uncharted equilibrium—one that placed it roughly at 20 million kilometres from Earth

at its closest approach. It was still distant enough to be safe, with minimal gravitational impacts, yet near enough that its brilliance in the night sky had permanently altered the way humanity saw the heavens.

Dr. Elena Marchant stood at the edge of her observatory's massive telescope, her breath catching as new data continued to stream in. Venus long considered a world of violent stasis, a prison of unyielding heat and pressure, had done the impossible. It had moved. Not as a slow drift over millennia, but in a sudden, cosmic pivot that defied existing models. She watched the live trajectory updates on her screen, still struggling to comprehend what had just unfolded.

"It's as if the solar system just performed an intricate ballet", she murmured. "Venus has found a new dance partner in Earth, but at a respectful distance."

Orbital Harmony: A New Scientific Frontier

The physics behind this cosmic minuet were fascinating. Venus had settled into a **near-resonant orbit** with Earth, completing **five orbits for every three of Earth's**—a delicate balance maintained by the interplay of gravitational forces between the Sun, Earth, and Venus. Though planetary resonances were common among moons and asteroids, such a synchronized motion between two worlds of this size was unprecedented.

The implications shattered previous assumptions about celestial mechanics. For centuries, planetary migrations had been considered slow, gradual affairs, unfolding over eons. But Venus had proven otherwise. Could planetary orbits be far more dynamic than previously imagined? Could other celestial bodies undergo similar rapid shifts? If so, what did that mean for planetary systems across the universe?

Dr. Marchant leaned closer to the data, her mind racing. The universe had just rewritten its own rules, revealing that planets were not bound to permanence. They could shift, adapt, and dance in ways humanity had never before conceived. Venus had defied expectations, and now, everything had changed.

The closer proximity of Venus had transformed it from an elusive inferno into an unparalleled scientific laboratory. No longer an unreachable mystery, it had become celestial proving ground, a world on humanity's cosmic doorstep. The greatest planetary minds of Earth had turned their full attention toward it, eager to decipher the secrets hidden beneath its swirling clouds.

Dr. Vernier, a leading planetary climatologist, stood before a packed conference at the International Astronomical Union, gesturing to a massive projection of Venus glowing in brilliant infrared. "We're seeing atmospheric structures we never could before," he said, his voice carrying over the hushed audience. "Venus's new orbit has turned it into a natural experiment, a living case study for greenhouse effects, atmospheric evolution, and planetary geology. This is a once-in-a-civilization opportunity."

Sarah Chen sat in the audience, furiously scribbling notes as Vernier spoke. She had spent her career modeling atmospheric changes, but nothing had prepared her for the sudden, real-time transformation of an entire planet. The shift in Venus's orbit had altered its exposure to solar radiation, and data was already revealing something extraordinary—its atmosphere was changing.

"We've long believed Venus's cloud systems were relatively stable," Vernier continued. "But the new orbital position is disrupting its upper atmosphere in ways we never predicted. The sulfuric acid clouds, once thought to be unchanging, are showing signs of dispersal and recombination."

Sarah's mind raced as she processed the implications. Venus's thick clouds trapped heat so efficiently that its surface remained a blistering 475 degrees Celsius—hot enough to melt lead. If those clouds were shifting, even slightly, what did that mean for the planet's climate over the next decades?

After the conference, she met with Dr. Yamamoto and a group of international researchers in a private briefing room, where live feeds from newly repositioned satellites filled the screens.

"Look at these readings," Yamamoto said, pointing to a real-time analysis. "Minor cooling detected in the upper troposphere. It's nothing drastic, but the numbers are there."

Vernier leaned in, adjusting his glasses. "If Venus's cloud layers thin even marginally, more infrared radiation could escape into space. Could that mean a long-term reduction in surface temperature?"

Sarah exhaled sharply, her eyes moving between the two scientists. "Are we saying Venus might be... changing?" The question hung in the air, weighted with implications no one had dared voice until now.

The room fell into profound silence. Each researcher seemed to hold their breath, aware they stood at the threshold of something unprecedented.

This possibility ignited a scientific renaissance focused on our sister planet. The European Space Agency unveiled plans for a revolutionary probe engineered to endure Venus's merciless conditions for months rather than hours. NASA and ISRO announced their partnership on an ambitious mission to deploy atmospheric drones that would map the shifting cloud formations with exquisite precision. China revealed blueprints for a floating research station— a concept dismissed as fantasy mere months ago but now pursued with fierce determination as space agencies worldwide raced to comprehend the transformation unfolding before them.

Philosophical and Spiritual Dimensions

The drive behind these efforts transcended pure scientific curiosity— it touched something deeper, more fundamental to our existence.

Venus had once mirrored Earth. Billions of years in the past, its surface might have shimmered with vast oceans, basked in gentle temperatures, perhaps even cradled the first stirrings of life. If a world could transform from paradise to inferno, and now possibly into something entirely new, what wisdom might this offer about Earth's own journey through cosmic time?

Sarah leaned back, her reflection ghosting across the monitor displaying Venus's luminous form. She saw the planet with new eyes—no longer a dead, unchanging sphere but a world in metamorphosis. Humanity had somehow earned the extraordinary privilege of witnessing planetary evolution in real time.

The Venus Event reverberated beyond laboratories and observatories, touching something primal in the human spirit. People who had glimpsed the abyss of extinction emerged not merely unharmed but profoundly altered in their perception of existence.

The universe had revealed itself not as the clockwork mechanism of scientific certainty but as something more mysterious—a living, evolving tapestry beyond human comprehension or control.

Houses of worship filled to overflowing across faiths and cultures. Seekers gathered to contemplate the significance of their narrow escape, searching for meaning in cosmic uncertainty. Some interpreted the Venus Event as communication from beyond—evidence that the universe possessed inherent balance, that disorder and harmony were eternal dance partners in creation's unfolding. From the Vatican, Pope Clement IX addressed a global audience, his voice carrying both solemnity and wonder as he spoke to a world forever changed.

"This is not the first time humankind has believed itself at the center of existence," he said. "But the heavens move as they will, unaffected by our beliefs or fears. Let this be a lesson in humility—to study, to understand, but never to assume we are the architects of the cosmos."

Others viewed the event as a warning, a stark reminder of human arrogance. A group of Buddhist monks in Kyoto gathered beneath the towering, golden glow of Venus, speaking softly among themselves. One, an elder named Hisato, turned to his students.

"We believed the planets were fixed in their courses," he said. "We believed we understood their ways. And yet, Venus moved. What else do we assume is certain, only to find it slipping through our grasp?"

The Venus Event was no longer a moment of terror, but of awe.

In the streets of Paris, Madrid, and São Paulo, artists took to the walls, painting murals of the cosmic ballet—the golden radiance of Venus woven into the fabric of the night, swirling with Earth in a silent, celestial waltz. Musicians composed symphonies inspired by the great shift, blending the haunting echoes of uncertainty with melodies of renewal. Poets wrote verses about a world reborn in fire and balance, their words carried across continents.

Sarah stood on the balcony of her apartment, staring at Venus, a beacon in the sky. It was no longer the harbinger of destruction, no longer an omen of the end. It had become a symbol of humanity's smallness, its curiosity, its resilience.

And for the first time in human memory, the stars no longer felt like distant, cold observers of our tiny lives.

The Night Sky Transformed

Our night sky had transformed irrevocably. Venus, now commanding the heavens at nearly twice its former size, dominated evening skies with a golden radiance that reshaped our experience of twilight and daybreak. Even in sprawling metropolises once blinded by their own artificial illumination, Venus pierced through the thickest urban haze, its brilliant presence impossible for even the most distracted city-dweller to overlook.

People who had never before noticed the heavens gathered spontaneously in parks and on rooftops, their borrowed or hastily purchased telescopes aimed at this celestial transformation. Venus's phases revealed themselves with unprecedented clarity, its swirling cloud patterns—hidden from human eyes throughout our entire existence—now dancing visibly across its face. Even without magnification, Venus appeared vibrant and dynamic, its atmospheric movements perceptible in real time, silently challenging humanity's perception of cosmic stillness.

On the windswept observation deck of Hawaii's Mauna Kea Observatory, a cluster of university students huddled around their professor, their breath misting in the crisp mountain air. Their voices mingled with the gentle whirring of equipment, each word carrying the unmistakable tremor of witnessing something profound.

"We're watching Venus evolve right before our eyes," breathed one young woman, her fingers delicately adjusting her telescope's focus, her face bathed in the golden light from above. "It's like seeing a living world instead of just some dead rock in space."

Dr. Elena Marchant overheard the comment and smiled, the lines at the corners of her eyes deepening. "It was always alive," she said softly, placing a hand on the student's shoulder. "We just weren't close enough—or perhaps paying enough attention—to see it."

Most remarkably, the dreaded consequences of Venus's orbital shift never materialized. The tidal disruptions that had haunted scientific predictions proved negligible. Earth's seasons continued their familiar rhythm. Our moon traced its ancient path, and the solar system maintained its delicate choreography.

Yet the very concept of cosmic stability had been forever altered in humanity's consciousness. Balance itself, Earth's inhabitants now understood, was merely a temporary state in an ever-shifting universe. Everything—from subatomic particles to massive celestial bodies—existed in perpetual evolution.

As the initial wave of panic receded like a tide, a new perspective washed over humanity. The Venus Event had accomplished what countless international summits and global crises had failed to do—unite Earth's scientific community in genuine, barrier-breaking collaboration. What began as a desperate race against extinction had blossomed into something far more profound: a coordinated human endeavor to comprehend planetary dynamics, atmospheric evolution, and celestial mechanics at a scale previously dismissed as beyond our reach.

Dr. Marchant would gather her students beneath the twilight sky, her arm extended toward that brilliant celestial jewel dominating the heavens. "We're just specks in the cosmos," she would tell them, her voice soft with wonder rather than diminished by insignificance. "But we're specks blessed with the capacity to observe, to learn, and to adapt. That gift—that hunger to understand—is what makes our brief existence so extraordinary."

The Venus Event embedded itself in human consciousness as a profound milestone in our collective journey. It served as a not-so-gentle but unmistakable reminder that even the paths of planets were not immutable as we once believed, that cosmic forces continued to unfold according to rhythms not yet fully grasped by our mathematics and theories.

Earth had gained something precious—a closer companion in its endless dance around the sun. Venus no longer hung as a distant point of light, a remote curiosity for specialists, but glowed as an active presence in humanity's evolving narrative. Night by night, it transformed into something more profound than a planetary body: it became a living symbol of transformation, resilience, and the boundless horizon of discovery that stretched before us.

What had initially sparked terror as a harbinger of doom had metamorphosed into something altogether different. Venus now stood as a beacon calling us toward deeper understanding, a mystery inviting exploration, a challenge that had awakened our finest qualities when faced with the unknown.

And each evening, as people from every corner of Earth lifted their gaze skyward—parents pointing it out to wide-eyed children, lovers making wishes upon it, scientists measuring its subtle changes—Venus seemed to whisper an ancient truth:

The universe has not finished surprising you, and perhaps it never will!

Chapter 7
The Turning Point

Image: iStock

The Cosmic Aftermath

Venus dominated our skies, no longer the feared messenger of our destruction but rather an intimate companion in our nightly darkness. Half a year had passed since those breathless days when humanity collectively waited—for either deliverance or oblivion. The end never arrived. What came instead was something far more nuanced and transformative: a fundamental reshaping of how we understood ourselves, our fragile blue world, and our place among the stars.

The planetary crisis had carved something new within the human spirit. People who had never before considered the cosmos now paused beneath twilight skies, their faces turned upward in quiet contemplation. Strangers shared telescopes in city parks, their differences temporarily dissolved by shared wonder. Children asked questions that had never occurred to previous generations.

Yet surviving catastrophe was not the same as resolving the deeper questions it had awakened. The immediate danger had passed, leaving humanity standing on unfamiliar ground. The universe had revealed itself as both more precarious and more wondrous than we had dared imagine.

Now that we knew the world would continue, a more profound question emerged from our collective soul: What would we do with this unexpected future we had been granted?

Dr. Emiliano Fuentes leaned back from the console, his brow furrowed. For days he had been charting Venus's position against high-fidelity orbital models, revisiting data that stretched back to the early Mariner and Venera flybys. The deviation was small—but unmistakable.

He stood up and walked to the whiteboard, sketching two sine curves: one for Venus's predicted ephemeris, the other for actual observations over the past twelve synodic cycles. The lines, once identical, now parted like a fork in the road.

Sarah Chen wandered through NASA's Houston headquarters, where the gentle hum of computers melded with hushed conversations echoing down the hallways. Everything felt different now. An electric urgency pulsed through every interaction, every knowing glance exchanged between scientists. Humanity had weathered the Venus crisis, yes—but survival had only birthed more profound questions. The universe was no longer the clockwork mechanism they'd once believed it to be. Venus had shifted—not merely in its celestial position, but in the collective human imagination.

"This isn't precession," he muttered. "It's migration."

Dr. Yamamoto appeared beside her, the weariness in his eyes mirroring her own bone-deep exhaustion. "What's it like, having a front-row seat to the complete rewriting of astrophysics?" he asked, the ghost of a smile playing at the corners of his mouth.

A colleague, Dr. Lhamo Yung, looked up. "Tidal forces?"

Sarah released a long breath, fingers absently combing through her hair. "Like we've barely scratched the surface of what's truly out there."

Fuentes shook his head. "Too fast. Too directional. It's not random drift—it's systemic. Intentional, almost."

They stepped into the main control room, where a constellation of screens displayed their technological reach—live satellite feeds, infrared imagery, and climate models—all hungrily focused on their celestial obsession. Venus. Never had the planet seemed so tantalizingly within reach, and the torrent of new discoveries was both exhilarating and overwhelming.

He hesitated, the marker still in his hand.

At the heart of this technological symphony, Dr. Elena Marchant hunched over fresh atmospheric readings, her face etched with the intensity of someone deciphering an ancient text. Sarah drew near, peering over her shoulder at the cascade of numbers and patterns.

The Grand Tack Hypothesis

"Have you ever heard of the Grand Tack Hypothesis?"

"The readings are finally stabilizing," Marchant murmured, almost to herself. "But look here—these cooling patterns in the upper atmosphere. It's subtle, like a whisper, but it's happening."

Lhamo blinked. "The early Jupiter model? Sure. Why?"

Sarah's pulse quickened as she read the latest reports. Venus's atmosphere was shifting. Fluctuations in cloud density, a drop in upper-atmosphere pressure, and minor—yet unprecedented—temperature variations. It wasn't a drastic change, but the implications were monumental.

He turned, voice quiet now. "Because I think we're seeing something like it. Again. A… Second Tack?"

"We're witnessing planetary evolution in real time," she murmured.

The words hung in the air like thunderclouds forming.

Yamamoto crossed his arms, eyes fixed on the screen. "And for the first time, we have the means to study it up close."

"You think Venus is changing orbit?"

Marchant tapped a command into her tablet, bringing up visual scans from NASA's orbital observatories. "We always assumed Venus was locked in climate stasis," she said. "But this? This suggests that planetary environments might be far more fluid than we ever imagined."

"I think it already has."

Sarah nodded, feeling the weight of the moment. Venus had rewritten everything they thought they knew. And now, it was up to them to understand what came next.

The World Reacts

On the streets of New York, Tokyo, London, and São Paulo, the world had transformed—not through destruction, but through perception. Billboards no longer pushed luxury brands or the latest tech gadgets. Instead, Venus was everywhere. It was painted across skyscrapers in towering murals, its golden glow woven into fashion designs, its image reimagined in film, poetry, and music.

Children, once enchanted by the Moon, now pointed excitedly at Venus, their young minds shaped by a world where the sky itself had changed. Teachers adjusted lesson plans, incorporating Venus into history, philosophy, and science, as if it had always been humanity's second sun.

But not all responses were poetic. The psychological weight of having a new celestial giant in the sky lingered in the human subconscious. Therapists saw a surge in patients struggling with an existential unease—an unnerving awareness of smallness.

"I can't explain it," one patient confided to Dr. Angela Martinez during a research interview. "It's not fear, exactly. It's more like… I was walking through life thinking I understood the world. And now, every time I look up, I'm reminded that I don't."

Others, however, found solace in the shift. If the cosmos could change and still find balance, maybe their own lives could, too. Spiritual movements flourished, blending science and philosophy, treating Venus as a cosmic lesson in adaptation.

Yet in some places, fear never truly faded. Conspiracy groups remained convinced that Venus's shift had been orchestrated by secretive world powers, evidence of a celestial experiment gone wrong. Some whispered that the planet was watching, an alien intelligence lurking beneath its thick clouds. Others predicted it was merely the first of many cosmic disruptions to come.

Governments, too, struggled to adjust. They had prepared for the catastrophe but not for survival. Diplomatic tensions flared over who controlled access to Venus, and what its changing climate might reveal.

Venus had moved, but in doing so, it had moved humanity as well—pulling minds, fears, and ambitions toward a sky that no longer belonged to the past.

In Washington, a closed-door meeting brought together world leaders, military strategists, and top scientists. The focus was no longer on why Venus had moved—but what to do with it now.

"The question is simple," a White House advisor stated, his voice measured but firm. "Do we treat Venus as a scientific opportunity or a strategic one?"

Silence descended upon the room like twilight, heavy with unspoken implications. The scientific community yearned for boundless collaboration—a sacred chance to unveil Venus's atmospheric secrets, geological mysteries, and the untold wonders hiding beneath those mesmerizing, swirling clouds. But the governments saw through different eyes entirely.

A planet that had dared to defy our cosmic understanding. A sister world so achingly close it had forever altered the way human hearts perceived the heavens above.

"Venus isn't just another celestial body anymore," the European Union official said, his voice carrying the weight of centuries of human ambition. "It's become something more intimate—a canvas for possibility. A testing ground for what we might become."

The room seemed to hold its collective breath.

"Perhaps Venus represents more than a mere scientific curiosity," suggested the Chinese defence strategist, her words carefully chosen yet resonating with raw human aspiration. "Perhaps it offers itself as humanity's first true planetary workshop? A place where we might test the boundaries of our cosmic influence?"

Dr. Elena Marchant, bearing the weathered wisdom of the scientific delegation, leaned forward. Her hands pressed against the table as if trying to steady a world spinning too quickly beneath her. "Terraforming Venus has lived in our dreams and stories," she said, her voice tinged with both wonder and caution. "And now you would transform those dreams into reality—turn Venus into a laboratory for our hopeful interference?"

The notion stirred something primal in every person present. For generations, terraforming had existed only in the imagination, a whispered possibility for children gazing at stars. But now, that whisper was growing into a chorus.

"If Venus herself is already in flux," an ESA scientist offered, unable to mask the tremor of excitement in her voice, "couldn't we join this cosmic dance? Couldn't we guide this transformation with gentle human hands?"

Marchant shook her head, her eyes carrying the burden of foresight. "And if our hands, however gentle, disturb a balance we don't yet understand?"

This passionate debate would echo through corridors of power for months, but one truth had already taken root in the human consciousness—our species would not turn away from Venus. Whether driven by the thirst for knowledge, the hunger for advantage, or something deeper in the human spirit, the pilgrimage to our sister planet had already begun in their hearts.

Despite the political chasms revealed in that moment, one truth shimmered with undeniable clarity—humanity's gaze, once fixed upon Venus, could never again look away!

NASA and Other Global Space Agencies 'Muscle-Up'!

Within months, an international coalition bloomed like a rare f and other lower, uniting the world's most sophisticated space agencies. NASA, ESA, Roscosmos, CNSA, ISRO, and others—once rivals who eyed each other across the void of space—now stood shoulder to shoulder beneath a single, hopeful banner: The Venus Initiative. For the first time in our tumultuous history, a planet's destiny had become a shared human tapestry, weaving together across borders, beyond ideologies, and healing ancient rivalries.

Sarah breathed in the electric anticipation filling NASA's packed briefing room, absorbing every detail as the mission unfurled before them. The sheer magnitude of their collective ambition left her breathless. The initiative's first phase—aptly named **Project Ascendancy**—would release a constellation of advanced probes designed to dance within Venus's clouds for unprecedented durations. These delicate mechanical emissaries would whisper back real-time secrets, tracking the moods and tempers of Venus's dense, temperamental atmosphere, alert for any signs that the planet's heart was continuing to beat with unexpected change. Venus had already surprised them once—if she was continuing her cosmic metamorphosis, humanity needed to bear witness.

The second phase, **Project Horizon**, reached even further into the realm of dreams. It would employ orbital imaging systems of such exquisite sensitivity that they bordered on the miraculous, all designed to finally unveil Venus in her naked glory. The very thought of witnessing Venus's surface in real time—mapping her endless volcanic plains stretching like frozen oceans, her mysterious highlands rising like questions, her deep canyons carved by unknowable forces—felt like stepping into a waking dream.

For centuries, Venus had remained a planet of whispers and imagination, her true face hidden behind an impenetrable veil of clouds. Now, for the first time, humanity would gaze upon her countenance with clear, adoring eyes.

But the real challenge lay ahead. The third phase, **Project Dawn**, would attempt the impossible landing, a robotic habitat on the surface. Venus's crushing pressure and infernal heat had destroyed every probe that had ever touched down. But if materials could be developed to survive there, to last more than minutes or hours, it would change everything. The groundwork for future human missions would finally be in place.

And then came the most radical of them all—**Project Aether**, the study of whether controlled planetary interventions could alter Venus's climate. Could its hellish conditions be shifted? Could a planet once thought unchangeable be nudged further along its new path? Scientists debated the ethics of such an experiment, while governments considered its long-term potential. It was no longer just about studying Venus. Some wanted to shape it.

Sarah glanced at Dr. Yamamoto, who sat beside her, arms crossed, his expression unreadable.

"We always thought Mars would be our first planetary frontier," he murmured.

Sarah exhaled, staring at the massive display screen where Venus glowed in haunting golden light.

"Turns out," she whispered, "it might be Venus instead."

Months later, the first mission was launched.

Across the world, people stopped what they were doing, eyes turning toward screens, waiting for history to unfold. **The Venus Ascendancy Probes** ignited and ascended into the sky, disappearing into the vastness of space, their course set toward the planet that had rewritten humanity's understanding of the cosmos. The event was broadcast across every channel, news networks replaying it endlessly, as if repetition could make the impossible feel real.

Angela Martinez sat in her Manhattan apartment, hands clasped together as she watched the coverage. For months, she had studied humanity's psychological response to Venus—fear, awe, paranoia, hope. But as the probes disappeared beyond Earth's atmosphere, she felt something else entirely.

A single tear slipped down her cheek, unbidden.

The fear had finally given way to something else.

In homes, schools, offices, and crowded public squares, people stood still. They weren't watching Venus with dread anymore.

They were watching with expectation.

Aboard NASA's mission control, Sarah Chen barely breathed as the first data streams from the probes arrived. Images began flooding in within hours of deployment—Venus's cloud formations, revealed in greater detail than ever before.

The thick, swirling atmosphere, once an impenetrable veil, now stretched across their monitors in stunning resolution.

Elena Marchant leaned closer to the display, her fingers dancing over the controls. "Look at this," she murmured, voice tinged with disbelief and wonder. "We're seeing details in Venus's cloud structure that we didn't even know existed."

The data continued pouring in. Infrared scans, revealing deeper thermal variations. Ultraviolet imaging, exposing the planet's turbulent winds in unprecedented clarity. Venus, once just a hazy silhouette in telescopes, was now an unfolding reality.

Sarah gazed at the screens, feeling each heartbeat reverberate through her chest like distant thunder. This moment—this profound, impossible moment—marked a turning point in human consciousness.

The Venus crisis had stripped away humanity's comfortable illusions, forcing our species to confront its own delicate existence in the cosmos, shattering the bedrock of everything we believed we understood about the universe we called home.

But now, something beautiful was emerging from that cosmic uncertainty.

It was compelling humanity to lift its collective gaze beyond the familiar horizon.

Venus, once dreaded as a harbinger of destruction, had transformed in the human imagination. She had become something altogether different, something luminous with possibility.

She had become our future

Chapter 8
The Venus Missions

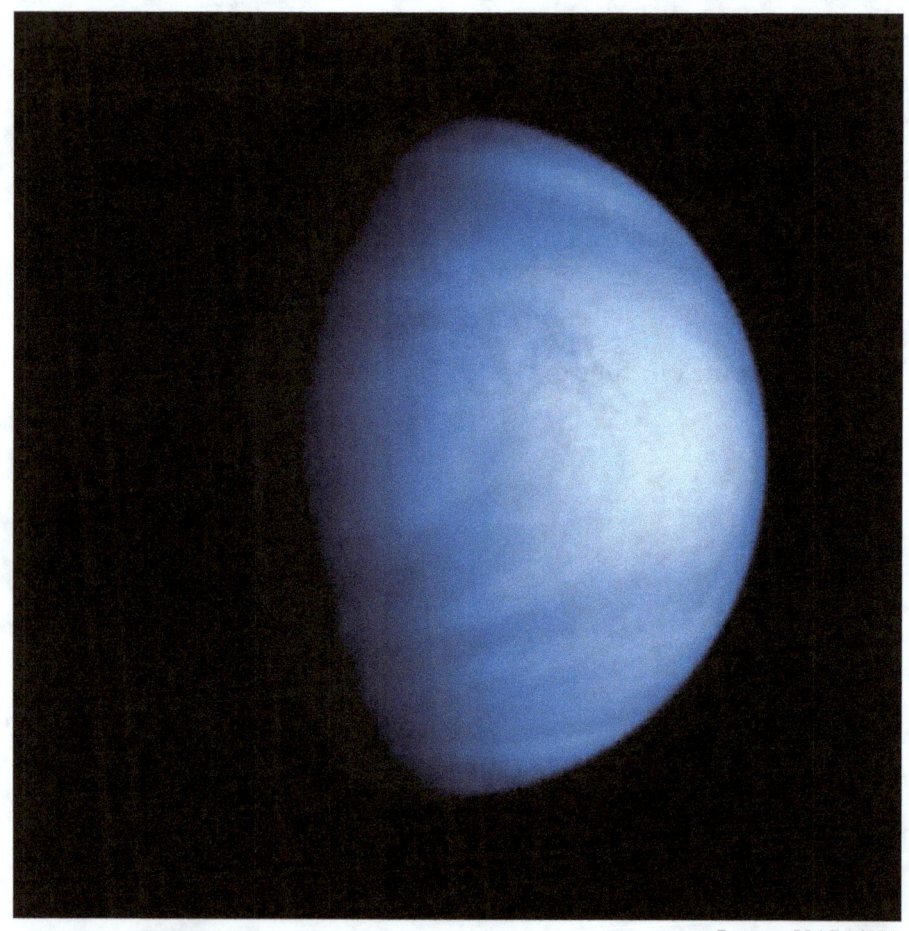

Image: NASA/JPL

This colourised picture of Venus was taken on February 14th, 1990, from a distance of almost 1.7 million miles, about 6 days after Galileo's closest approach to the planet. It has been colorized to a bluish hue to emphasize subtle contrasts in the cloud markings and to indicate that it was taken through a violet filter, as seen by the SSI instrument on Galileo.

Daedalus I: Humanity's Boldest Voyage

The world watched in silence as the **Daedalus I** mission prepared for its final approach to Venus. For months, the spacecraft had travelled through the void, its crew adjusting to life in the sterile confines of their reinforced habitat module. But now, as they prepared for the descent, the weight of what they were about to do pressed down on them heavier than the planet's crushing atmosphere.

No human had ever dared come this close to Venus. No manned mission had ever attempted to breach its dense cloud cover. Every probe ever sent had been either obliterated by heat or crushed by pressure within minutes of touching down. Yet here they were, six astronauts about to make history—or become footnotes in humanity's quest to understand its nearest planetary neighbour.

Mission Control — NASA, Houston

Sarah Chen sat in the dim glow of a hundred monitors, heart pounding in sync with the rhythmic beeping of telemetry readouts. The room was packed—NASA scientists, ESA engineers, Russian flight coordinators, ISRO specialists—all watching with unblinking intensity. The entire Venus Initiative depended on what happened in the next few hours.

Coffee cups sat cold and forgotten. No one had slept properly for days. The mission had been years in the making, billions in funding, and countless careers staked on its success.

"Daedalus, we're reading stable telemetry," she said into her headset, forcing her voice to remain steady. "Confirming orbital insertion burn in T-minus three minutes."

A brief pause crackled across the comms before Commander Jason Iwata's voice responded. "Copy, Houston. Burn sequence locked in." His voice betrayed nothing of the tension they all felt.

Dr. Yamamoto, the project's lead scientist, leaned forward beside Sarah, his eyes reflecting the blue glow of the screens. "If this works," he whispered, "we rewrite every textbook on planetary science."

71

"*If* is the operative word," Sarah replied, then keyed her mic again. "Roger, Daedalus. Stand by for atmosphere entry sequence."

Sarah exhaled, gripping the edge of the console. This was the moment. If the calculations were off by even a fraction of a degree, the ship would burn up or be torn apart before it reached its target altitude. Venus didn't tolerate mistakes. The planet had devoured every lander since the Soviet Venera missions, none lasting more than 127 minutes on its hellish surface.

Into the Venusian Maelstrom

The room fell silent as the countdown began.

Commander Jason Iwata adjusted his harness as the ship trembled, preparing to fire its aerobraking thrusters. His stomach knotted with a mixture of excitement and fear. After sixteen years as an astronaut, he thought he knew what to expect from space. Venus was proving him wrong with every passing second.

The upper atmosphere of Venus was their destination—a zone where temperatures hovered around 50°C, relatively mild compared to the inferno below. This was where the **Zephyr Research Platform**, an advanced floating atmospheric station, would be deployed. If they succeeded, it would be humanity's first long-term presence in the Venusian skies.

"Systems check," he ordered, scanning his crew. Dr. Elena Rassadov, their mission specialist, nodded confidently. Lt. Michael Chan, their pilot, gave a thumbs up. Dr. Aisha Okafor, their atmospheric chemist, was already poring over preliminary data. They had trained together for three years for this moment.

"We're green for descent," said Elena, fingers dancing across her console. "Heat shielding engaged. Automated stabilization online."

Through the small viewport, Venus loomed—a brilliant white-gold sphere against the blackness of space. From this distance, it appeared almost peaceful, its cloud tops reflecting sunlight like a marble sculpture. Iwata knew better. Beneath that deceptive beauty lurked an environment more hostile than any place humans had ever ventured.

"Copy," Iwata said. "We begin our approach in three... two... one."

The thrusters ignited in perfect synchronization, tilting Daedalus into its descent trajectory. The ship lurched violently as it slammed into the upper edge of Venus's thick clouds. The pressure mounted instantly, gravity pulling at them harder than they'd experienced on Earth.

"Hull temperature rising," Lt. Chan reported, his voice tight. "Within acceptable parameters, but climbing faster than projected."

Through the viewport, a world unlike anything they had imagined unfolded.

The clouds were not still; they churned violently, streaked with huge lightning bolts. Yellow sulfuric mist billowed around them, illuminated by the faint glow of the sun fighting through the dense atmosphere. They were descending into a storm that had raged for millions of years.

"My God," whispered Aisha, abandoning scientific detachment as she pressed against her restraints to see better. "The atmosphere is... *changing*."

Iwata barely had time to react before an unexpected turbulence sent the ship spinning off-axis. Warning alarms blared throughout the cabin. Loose items broke free, clattering against walls and floating in the temporarily weightless environment.

"Stabilizers, now!" he barked.

"Engaging gyros—compensating," Elena shouted over the cacophony of alerts, her fingers flying across emergency protocols. Sweat beaded on her forehead despite the climate controls.

The ship groaned in protest as the thrusters fired again, struggling against the thickening atmosphere. Outside, visibility was almost non-existent. Venus was swallowing them whole.

"Structural integrity at ninety-two percent," Chan reported, his usual calm demeanour showing cracks. "We're being pulled into a cyclonic formation."

Iwata had been prepared for challenges, but not this. The simulations had never captured the raw, primeval power of Venus's atmosphere. It wasn't just hostile—it was *alive* with energy and motion.

"The atmosphere," Aisha said, staring at her readings, "it's not stable like we thought. Look at these pressure differences—the cloud layers are breaking apart and reforming in ways that shouldn't be possible."

Mission Control — Houston

Sarah gripped her headset so tightly her knuckles whitened. "Daedalus, we're seeing erratic movement on our end. Status?"

A burst of static, then Iwata's voice came through, broken and distorted. "Atmospheric turbulence is worse than predicted. Maintaining altitude. Sensors are... Houston, we're picking up something unusual."

Sarah glanced at the telemetry feed. Readings were fluctuating. Venus's pressure, temperature, and wind speeds were shifting in real time—far beyond what had ever been recorded. The planet was reacting to their presence, as if disturbed from a long slumber.

Around her, technicians exchanged worried glances. Dr. Yamamoto leaned forward, knuckles pressed to his lips.

"Define 'unusual,' Daedalus," she said, fighting to keep her voice level for the sake of everyone in the room.

Elena's voice cut in, breathless with excitement or fear, perhaps both. "Infrared scans... are detecting surface heat anomalies. Active heat signatures. This isn't ancient geological activity. This is happening now."

Sarah's blood ran cold. The implications were staggering. "Repeat that, Daedalus."

"We're detecting live volcanic activity—repeat, Venus is currently erupting."

The control room erupted in a flurry of activity. Monitors were recalibrated, data streams reassessed. What had begun as a milestone mission of exploration was rapidly evolving into something much more profound—a fundamental shift in humanity's understanding of planetary geology.

"All secondary systems focus on those heat signatures," Dr. Yamamoto ordered, suddenly animated. "Get me thermal mapping, spectroscopic analysis, everything!"

The Zephyr Research Platform Deployment

As the Daedalus stabilized, the crew worked with practiced precision to deploy the Zephyr Research Platform, an autonomous floating station that would drift in Venus's atmosphere for months, collecting data on the volcanic activity unfolding below. Unlike previous probes, Zephyr was designed to endure. It would hover in the middle layers of the atmosphere, buoyed by an atmosphere of solid carbon dioxide, using solar power to sustain itself, sending back high-resolution imagery and atmospheric readings.

The deployment bay opened, exposing the compact research platform to Venus's atmosphere. Elena monitored the sequence, her face illuminated by status lights.

"Main inflation sequence initiated," she reported as the platform's sophisticated aerogel balloons began to expand, designed to keep the station aloft in Venus's dense atmosphere.

"Instrument array coming online," Aisha added, watching as the platform's delicate sensors powered up one by one, protected by special ceramic composites that could withstand the caustic environment.

"Zephyr deployed," Elena confirmed finally, exhaling in relief. "Tracking stable altitude at 55 kilometers above surface."

Through the ship's external cameras, they could see the golden sky roiling beneath them, the vast plains of Venus momentarily illuminated by the glow of lava flows erupting from deep fissures in the surface. The landscape was a cracked, hellish tableau, lit from below by molten rock that flowed like liquid fire across the barren plains.

"This planet was never dead," Iwata murmured, awestruck by the primordial display of planetary power. "We just weren't looking close enough."

"Preliminary readings suggest multiple active volcanic sites," Aisha reported, her voice trembling with scientific excitement. "We're seeing significant sulphur dioxide emissions... and something else..." She paused, checking her readings again. "The atmosphere is shifting—there are zones where pressure is fluctuating, as if the entire system is trying to find a new equilibrium."

Lt. Chan shook his head in disbelief. "What does this mean for our understanding of terrestrial planets?"

"Everything," Elena replied, eyes wide. "It means everything."

Unexpected Discoveries

As Daedalus I ascended from Venus's atmosphere, the Zephyr platform continued its silent watch, sensors recording every subtle shift in the planet's volatile environment. What they were witnessing wasn't just a geological curiosity—it was a window into Earth's possible future.

"If Venus is still geologically active," Dr. Yamamoto said, reviewing the initial data back at Mission Control, "then we need to rethink our models of planetary evolution."

Sarah nodded, her mind racing with the implications. "We've always viewed Venus as a cautionary tale—a runaway greenhouse effect with no possibility of reversal. But if these atmospheric fluctuations continue..."

"Then maybe planetary climates aren't as permanent as we thought," Elena finished, joining them via video link from Daedalus. "What if Venus isn't just a warning? What if it's a cycle? What if, during certain periods, Venus was less extreme—maybe even capable of supporting liquid water?"

The room fell silent as the weight of that possibility settled over them. For decades, they had assumed Venus was locked in a permanent catastrophe, a runaway greenhouse effect with no end. But what if they were wrong?

What if planets could recover from extreme conditions?

What if Venus held secrets that might help reverse Earth's own climate trajectory?

Rewriting Planetary Science

The discovery sent shockwaves through the scientific community. Venus had been assumed to be a static, hostile world, but now, it was clear—it was still evolving. Its interior was active. Its atmosphere was changing. The implications extended beyond Venus itself—to Mars, to exoplanets, to Earth's own future.

Within hours, world leaders were convening urgent meetings. The Venus Initiative shifted from a research mission to a priority planetary study effort. New probes were being greenlit. The ESA announced an immediate acceleration of its VERITAS mission, and China proposed a long-term orbital station to monitor Venus permanently.

In the corner of Mission Control, Sarah Chen watched as the first high-resolution images from Zephyr flooded in—active volcanoes on a planet thought to be geologically dormant. Each frame rendered previous models obsolete. Decades of textbooks would need rewriting.

"We never imagined this," Dr. Yamamoto said, voice hushed with wonder. "All these years, we thought Venus was Earth's dead sister— a cautionary tale of runaway greenhouse effect. But it's not dead. It's just... different."

Sarah nodded, understanding the weight of what they were witnessing. "And if Venus is still active after all this time..."

"Then planetary evolution is far more complex than we believed," Yamamoto finished. "It means planets don't follow linear paths. They can change course, even billions of years into their life cycles."

Sarah Chen knew this was bigger than any single mission. Venus had proven that planets could change—quickly, violently, unexpectedly. And if Venus could change, what did that mean for Earth's future?

"We've rewritten the rules of planetary science," Dr. Yamamoto said, standing beside her. "But now we need to ask—what comes next?"

Venusian Legacy.

As the crew of Daedalus I prepared for their journey back to Earth, Commander Iwata took one last look at the golden world below. "We came expecting to find a warning," he murmured. "Instead, we found something still fighting to exist."

Venus had been pushed to extremes, its water gone, its atmosphere a crushing blanket of carbon dioxide and acid clouds. But beneath that hostile exterior, its heart still beat. Magma still flowed through its veins. Its atmosphere still shifted and churned, perhaps searching for a new balance that had eluded it for billions of years.

"I think we've been looking at Venus all wrong," Aisha said, standing beside him. "We saw it as Earth's failed twin, but maybe it's just at a different stage of its journey."

The implications for Earth were profound. If planetary atmospheres could change this dramatically—either toward catastrophe or away from it—then Earth's climate crisis took on new dimensions. It wasn't just about preventing disaster; it was about understanding the complex, long-term cycles that governed planetary evolution.

Sarah turned back to the monitor, watching as Daedalus I began its ascent, leaving behind the roiling clouds of Earth's twin. The spacecraft looked tiny against the vast backdrop of Venus—a fragile emissary from one world to another.

As Zephyr transmitted its first complete atmospheric analysis, scientists around the world fell silent in collective awe. Venus wasn't just a failed Earth. It was its own world, with its own story still unfolding.

Venus had kept its secrets for billions of years.

But now, they were listening.

And what they heard would change humanity's place in the cosmos forever.

Chapter 9
The Cost of Survival

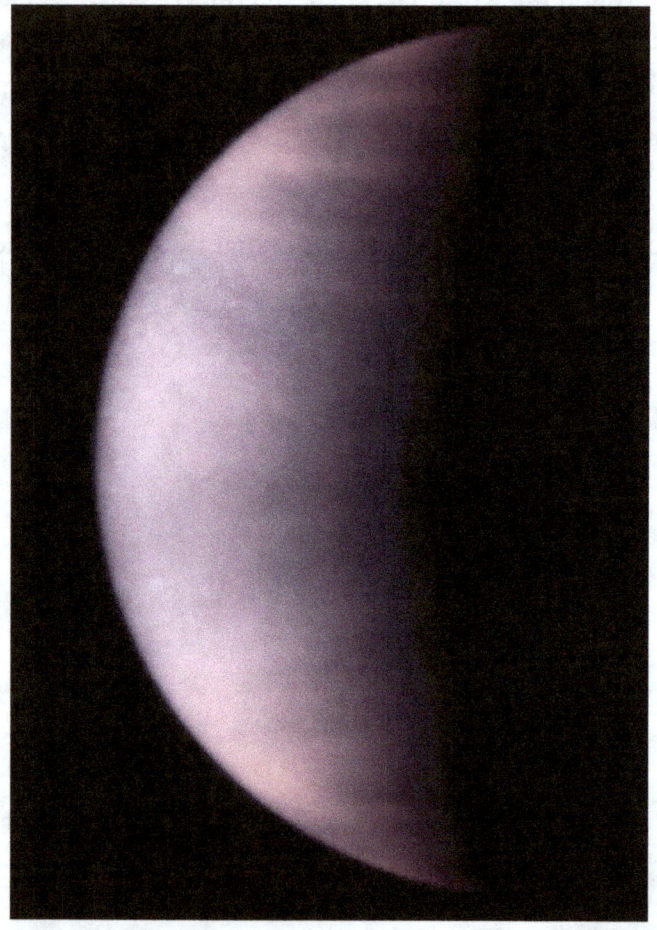

Image: NASA/JPL

This is a NASA Hubble Space Telescope ultraviolet-light image of the planet Venus, taken on January 24, 1995, when Venus was at a distance of 70.6 million miles (113.6 million kilometres) from Earth. False colour has been used to enhance cloud features.

As Venus is closer to the Sun than Earth, the planet appears to go through phases, like the Moon. When Venus swings close to Earth, the planet's disk appears to grow in size, but changes from a full disk to a crescent.

Sisters Across Time

Sarah Chen sat alone in her office, the soft glow of monitors casting ethereal shadows across her face as she gazed at the latest transmission from Daedalus I. Venus revealed herself in haunting splendour—a world wreathed in passionate fury, her skies a tapestry of swirling sulfuric acid clouds, her true face barely visible beneath that thick, smothering veil.

She looked like mankind's most ancient nightmare given form.

And yet, surrounded by Mission Control's reverent, mechanical heartbeat, Sarah couldn't escape a thought that wound itself around her heart with cold fingers: Was she witnessing Earth's mirror, placed across time?

With a breath that caught in her throat, she called forth the latest climate reports from NASA's Earth Observatory. The data unfurled beside Venus's fierce countenance, telling a parallel story with unflinching honesty—carbon dioxide rising like humanity's fever, temperatures breaking records not with triumph but with dread, wildfires consuming landscapes with the hunger of ancient gods, and seas patiently reclaiming coastal homes one heartbeat at a time.

Venus had once cradled gentler dreams, the stones of science suggested. Billions of years past, her skies might have echoed our own blue sanctuary, with oceans that sang beneath twin suns, air that welcomed life's first breath, perhaps even the tender awakening of consciousness. But something had shattered this fragile balance. A greenhouse effect had transformed this sister into a burning testament, trapping heat beneath her clouded skin until her surface wept molten metal.

For too long, humanity had held Venus as merely a cautionary fable—a cosmic tragedy, an unfortunate sibling's fate, a scholarly footnote in the margins of our own story.

What if we were fundamentally wrong? What if Venus wasn't merely some abstract planetary anomaly—but was actually transmitting a message we had been too blind to discern?

"You know, we've always characterized Venus as an enigma," said Dr. Elena Marchant as she entered the room, clutching her tablet with a white-knuckled intensity that betrayed her outward composure. Her gaze drifted to the main display where Venus raged with its ceaseless atmospheric storms, her expression carried a deep, thoughtful seriousness that went beyond simple scientific interest."

"But perhaps the mystery isn't in understanding its mechanics, but in acknowledging what it signifies—a premonition writ large across our celestial neighbourhood."

Sarah sighed and massaged her temples, fatigue radiating through her skull in persistent waves that had become her constant companion these past weeks.

"If Venus is indeed offering a warning," she replied with quiet resignation, "we may have already squandered the luxury of prevention."

Elena settled beside Sarah, their shoulders nearly touching in the dim light. She activated her tablet, illuminating the space between them with vibrant climatological models—oceanic blues fading to alarming crimson patterns that told a story neither wished to verbalise.

"The revelations from our Venus studies are... troubling at best," Elena said, her voice diminishing to little more than a whisper. "We had presumed Venus represented a static endpoint, the culmination of a runaway greenhouse effect that had reached thermodynamic equilibrium. But the data defies that assumption. The planet continues to evolve, and the trajectory is disconcerting."

Sarah's expression contracted with profound concern. "That contradicts all established models."

Indeed," Elena nodded, her fingers tracing the contours of thermal anomalies highlighted on her screen. "And these same accelerated transformations... they're manifesting in Earth's systems at an alarming rate." She lowered her gaze, examining her hands as if they might hold some solution. "It's as though the fundamental principles of planetary climate dynamics we've relied upon are proving inadequate—or worse, fundamentally flawed."

A weighty silence enveloped them, thick with unspoken implications. The central question hovered between them—too ominous to articulate yet impossible to ignore.

They both recalled Earth as it once was—verdant forests stretching toward pristine horizons, air that filled lungs with vitality rather than toxins, and summers that invited rather than threatened. Such memories seemed increasingly distant, like half-remembered dreams from a more innocent age.

Sarah leaned toward her terminal, apprehension evident in the tight lines around her eyes as she scrutinized the accumulating data.

"Elena," Sarah said without shifting her gaze from the monitor, "I've been contemplating something rather unsettling. The prevailing theory suggests Venus underwent its transformation gradually—over geological timescales spanning millions of years. But what if that assumption is fundamentally incorrect? What if the transformation occurred at a far more accelerated rate?"

Elena halted her analysis abruptly, her scientific objectivity momentarily eclipsed by the maternal instinct that envisioned a world her children would inherit.

"Are you suggesting our temporal projections for Earth's climate destabilization might be drastically compressed?"

Sarah nodded, the gravity of her hypothesis settling between them like lead. "I believe we may be measuring our remaining window for effective intervention in decades rather than centuries."

They regarded one another across the dimly lit space, the implications transforming this ordinary exchange into a pivotal moment of recognition—a devastating epiphany that fundamentally altered their perception of humanity's predicament.

Elena's expression hardened with sudden clarity. "And here we are, directing unprecedented resources toward Venus exploration... when perhaps our most urgent priority should be Earth's preservation."

Sarah returned her attention to the displays, where Venus gleamed with malevolent beauty. The data streams and spectral analyses no longer represented mere scientific curiosities—they had metamorphosed into prophetic warnings, a planetary harbinger of Earth's potential fate should humanity's course remain unaltered.

Venus had already passed beyond salvation. Would Earth's trajectory follow the same catastrophic path?

Global Responses / The Human Cost

Meanwhile, across the globe, public discourse had expanded beyond Venus's anomalous orbital behaviour and the mysterious cosmic signal that had captivated scientific attention for months. Now, a more profound debate was emerging—one that questioned humanity's priorities in the face of existential crisis.

Nations were allocating unprecedented financial resources toward Venus research. Space agencies received funding that dwarfed their previous budgets. Corporate entities launched proprietary missions to exploit the scientific goldmine that Venus had become. The academic community had pivoted en masse, redirecting intellectual capital toward understanding our sister planet with an intensity that bordered on obsession.

Venus had transcended its former status as a mere celestial body, becoming the focal point of humanity's collective attention.

Yet as humanity's gaze remained fixated upward, a crucial question reverberated with increasing urgency: Shouldn't our primary focus be directed downward—toward addressing the ecological degradation of our own planetary home before it's irreversibly compromised?

At the United Nations, the atmosphere pulsed with palpable tension. World leaders, eminent scientists, and passionate activists had assembled for an emergency summit. The grand chamber, typically characterized by diplomatic restraint and measured discourse, now crackled with undisguised urgency. National flags hung in symmetrical rows, silent witnesses to deliberations that would shape humanity's trajectory. Journalists positioned discreetly along the perimeter captured every word for the billions who watched with mounting anxiety, desperate for reassurance or direction amid cosmic uncertainty.

A European delegate rose first, his countenance bearing the unmistakable weight of grave responsibility. He gestured toward the central display where climate models glowed in alarming crimson patterns, illustrating Earth's accelerating biosphere degradation. His voice, though controlled, vibrated with barely contained emotion. "We stand amid an unprecedented climate catastrophe," he stated, his words hanging in the charged atmosphere. "Coastal populations face imminent displacement. Agricultural systems are collapsing in multiple regions. Fresh water access diminishes daily. How can we justify allocating trillions to Venus exploration while our own planet's life-support systems unravel before our eyes?"

Murmurs of agreement rippled through the assembly—heads nodding in solemn affirmation, others cradled in hands of despair.

An American scientist approached the podium next, his weathered hands gripping its edges with the quiet intensity of someone whose dire predictions had repeatedly materialized. Fatigue etched deep lines around his eyes, yet they burned with conviction. "Venus is not merely a distant scientific curiosity," he declared, scanning the assembled dignitaries. "It represents Earth's potential future—the culmination of a runaway greenhouse effect. That planet underwent transformations that mirror the very processes we've initiated here. If we can decipher Venus's evolutionary pathway, perhaps we can prevent Earth from following the same catastrophic trajectory."

The assembly fractured along visible ideological lines, the division palpable in the charged atmosphere.

Economists presented sobering analyses of climate-induced economic collapse—agricultural failures, infrastructural destruction, mass migration, and the staggering costs of adaptation versus prevention. Space agency representatives countered with impassioned arguments for continued Venus research, insisting that salvation might lie in the insights gleaned from our planetary neighbour.

Beyond the conference hall's fortified perimeter, multitudes gathered in public squares—ordinary citizens whose futures hung in the balance of decisions made by those within. Their banners fluttered in the unseasonably warm breeze, bearing messages that ranged from demands for immediate carbon neutrality to appeals for enhanced reforestation initiatives. Their collective voice rose above partisan divisions, unified by an existential imperative that transcended traditional political allegiances.

Meanwhile, in climate-controlled boardrooms and at private launch facilities removed from public scrutiny, the planet's economic elite pursued extraterrestrial contingencies. For these privileged few, Venus represented not a cautionary example but a strategic opportunity—perhaps even an insurance policy should Earth's habitability continue its precipitous decline.

Rewriting Planetary Science

Sarah Chen observed the proceedings with the analytical detachment of a scientist juxtaposed against the visceral concern of a global citizen. She absorbed the passionate arguments from each faction, recognizing the validity inherent in their respective positions. Yet the deepening polarization troubled her profoundly, for it threatened to fragment humanity precisely when unified action was most crucial.

Because the fundamental question wasn't about choosing between Earth and Venus.

It was about ensuring humanity's continued existence—preserving not only our biological survival but the essence of what defines us as a species: our capacity for compassion, our boundless curiosity, and our unique ability to unite in the face of existential challenges.

Dr. Elena Marchant sat adjacent to Sarah, watching as the assembly devolved into increasingly fractious discourse—voices rising in volume while diminishing in receptivity, accusations supplanting collaboration, ideological entrenchment replacing intellectual flexibility.

Elena released a weary sigh, shaking her head almost imperceptibly. "They could sustain this rhetorical stalemate indefinitely," she whispered, her tone weighted with melancholy. "And while they engage in philosophical duelling, our remaining window for meaningful intervention continues to contract—time we simply cannot afford to squander if we hope to address both Earth's deterioration and Venus's mysteries."

Sarah pressed her fingertips against her throbbing temples, attempting to alleviate the persistent headache that had become her constant companion. "I've ceased viewing this as a binary choice," she responded softly, as though speaking to herself rather than her colleague. "Somehow, we must forge a path that encompasses both Earth's preservation and Venus's exploration. The fate of one is inextricably linked to our understanding of the other."

Elena turned to regard her friend, her expression revealing both profound concern and unresolved questions. "And if such a harmonious integration proves fundamentally unattainable?"

Sarah fell silent, the inquiry hovering between them, laden with all its unspoken implications. What possible response could adequately address the magnitude of their predicament without surrendering to despair?

The truth crystallized within her consciousness like a glacial formation—solid, immovable, and fundamentally disturbing.

If Earth's biosphere deteriorated beyond recovery, rendering our planet inhospitable to human civilization... Venus might represent humanity's final recourse.

But if Venus remained the hellish inferno, it had always been—if we proved incapable of transforming it into a viable habitat—then humanity would face extinction without recourse or remedy.

It was astonishing how rapidly theoretical speculation had transmuted into desperate pragmatism. Merely twelve months prior, the concept of Venus terraforming existed solely within speculative fiction and theoretical astrobiology—the kind of fascinating thought experiment scientists might explore over conference refreshments, fully aware that such possibilities lay centuries beyond current technological capabilities.

Now? Governmental authorities were earnestly debating resource allocation toward such initiatives. Engineers were drafting preliminary designs. Ordinary citizens were contemplating the implications.

What had once occupied the exclusive domain of imaginative fiction had somehow, terrifyingly, become the most consequential question confronting our species:

Where will humanity reside when Earth can no longer sustain us?

Venus had once been a paradisiacal world that, geological evidence suggested, might have harboured oceans, a temperate atmosphere, and conceivably the potential for biological development. But some critical threshold had been crossed. Its runaway greenhouse effect had transformed it into a planetary-scale cautionary tale of atmospheric destabilization.

If Venus's fate had once been preventable, could it now be reversible?

The proposals proliferated with audacious ambition. Certain scientific contingents advocated for atmospheric seeding with genetically engineered extremophile microorganisms—bacteria specifically designed to metabolize carbon dioxide and generate oxygen as a byproduct.

Others promoted the implementation of reflective atmospheric aerosols that could potentially reduce planetary temperature by redirecting solar radiation back into space. The most visionary proponents suggested orchestrating controlled asteroid impacts to deliver water and recalibrate Venus's chemical composition—an undertaking that would unfold across centuries or millennia.

Some perceived these initiatives as humanity's boldest frontier. Others condemned them as hubris of unprecedented magnitude.

Dr. Yamamoto had emerged as perhaps the most vocal critic. "We are not cosmic architects," he had declared during a global climate summit, his voice cutting through the assembly with crystalline clarity. "We have barely begun to comprehend Venus's evolutionary trajectory, yet we presume to reverse it? We must abandon this dangerous illusion of omnipotence over forces that transcend our understanding."

Elena, however, represented the opposing philosophical position. Before an assembly of the world's preeminent scientists, her voice resonated with unwavering conviction. "Venus represents the ultimate manifestation of runaway climate destabilization. If we can mitigate even a fraction of its hostile conditions, we demonstrate something revolutionary that planetary trajectories aren't immutable. That ecological salvation remains possible, even from the most extreme environmental degradation."

The ethical considerations proved impossible to disentangle from practical concerns.

Venus terraforming would require multi-generational commitment, employing technological capabilities that currently existed only in theoretical frameworks. Meanwhile, Earth's climate destabilization accelerated relentlessly.

Oceanic levels rose with unprecedented rapidity, exceeding even the most pessimistic projections. Extreme meteorological events transformed from anomalous occurrences into seasonal inevitabilities. Agricultural productivity declined precipitously, triggering food scarcity that threatened geopolitical stability.

A United Nations representative struck the conference table with barely contained frustration. "Billions endure suffering today. How can we rationalize committing astronomical resources toward Venus when immediate humanitarian crises demand resolution here?"

Lessons for Earth

Yet one argument remained impossible to dismiss.

If Earth's habitability continued its decline, Venus represented the only other planetary body in our solar system with the appropriate mass, gravity, and potential to eventually support human civilization.

Mars remained fundamentally unsuitable—too cold, too barren, possessing insufficient gravity and atmospheric pressure, and too distant for large-scale colonization.

Venus—if its extreme environment could be incrementally modified—potentially offered humanity's second chance.

Was the possibility, however remote, worth pursuing?

Sarah and Elena sat opposite one another in a darkened NASA conference room, their faces illuminated by the blue glow of comparative planetary models displaying Venus's hellscape juxtaposed against Earth's deteriorating biosphere.

"I fear we're replicating our fundamental error," Sarah said, her voice barely audible above the environmental systems' gentle hum. She gestured toward the dual displays showing Venus's toxic atmosphere alongside Earth's intensifying carbon saturation. "What if our intervention in Venus's atmosphere merely replicates the same anthropogenic catastrophe we've initiated here?"

Elena inhaled deeply, choosing her words with deliberate care. "I don't perceive our efforts as abandoning Earth," she said with measured precision. "Rather, I see it as prudent contingency planning. We continue working to reverse Earth's climate degradation but simultaneously develop alternatives should those efforts prove insufficient."

Sarah's fingers drummed a restless rhythm against the polished conference table. "Or perhaps," she countered with renewed conviction, "we should redirect those immense resources toward addressing the environmental crisis we've created here—on the only planet currently capable of supporting human civilization."

Silence enveloped them like a physical presence.

"I believe it may already be too late," Elena said softly, leaning back as exhaustion etched deeper lines around her eyes. "Polar ice dissolution accelerates exponentially. Coastal metropolitan areas face imminent inundation. Weather patterns destabilize beyond predictive modelling. Food production systems collapse in regions previously considered agricultural strongholds. We're witnessing cascading system failures across multiple ecological domains simultaneously."

Sarah's brow furrowed in profound concentration. "So your solution is to stake everything on Venus? A planet that may remain permanently uninhabitable—while Earth remains potentially salvageable?"

"I'm not advocating abandonment," Elena clarified, her voice softening with genuine concern. "I'm suggesting we pursue parallel strategies. Continue Earth remediation efforts with unwavering commitment, while simultaneously developing contingency plans should those efforts prove insufficient. What if, despite our most determined interventions, Earth's climate passes irreversible tipping points? What if Venus represents our only remaining option?"

Sarah contemplated the displays—Earth's familiar azure sphere with its emerald continents juxtaposed against Venus's golden inferno. Two planets. Two potential futures. Neither outcome guaranteed, both hanging in delicate balance.

Sarah's gaze shifted between the twin monitors before her—one displaying Earth's familiar blues and greens now increasingly marred by atmospheric disruption, the other revealing Venus's golden tempest that had once mirrored our own world's conditions.

Two worlds.

Two potential futures.

And humanity stood at the ultimate crossroads, compelled to determine which path they would commit to forging.

Epilogue I
A New Perspective

Sometime later, the scientific advantages of Venus' closer orbit became apparent. The expanded ability to study our sister planet resulted in ground-breaking findings on planetary formation, atmospheric dynamics, and world evolution. The increased proximity enabled robotic research, resulting in a new series of Venus missions that transformed our understanding of terrestrial planets.

But perhaps the most important lesson was not about Venus, but about Earth.

Venus used to be very similar to Earth. Geological data suggests that oceans and a moderate environment existed billions of years ago. But something happened. A runaway greenhouse effect converted it into a hellscape, with surface temperatures capable of melting lead and atmospheric pressure roughly 100 times that of Earth. Venus was a warning, a glimpse of what may happen if humanity continued to exceed Earth's limitations.

An artist's impression of the transformation of Venus from Earth-like to hell-like. *(Credit: NASA's Goddard Space Flight Centre)*

Venus: A Mirror to Earth's Future

As scientists investigated Venus' newly accessible atmosphere and surface, a profound realization crystallized: Earth was following an eerily similar environmental trajectory. The mirror Venus held before us reflected not just scientific curiosity, but a stark vision of a possible future.

Venus had once been Earth's true twin—geological evidence suggested it had harboured oceans, moderate temperatures, and possibly the conditions for life billions of years ago. But a critical threshold had been crossed. A runaway greenhouse effect had transformed this once-habitable world into a hellscape of molten metal temperatures and crushing atmospheric pressure. This wasn't merely academic knowledge anymore—it had become humanity's most urgent lesson.

The climate patterns that had doomed Venus were disturbingly recognizable in Earth's own changing systems: rapidly increasing carbon dioxide levels, intensifying storm cycles, accelerating glacial melt, and record-shattering temperature extremes. Venus wasn't just a neighbouring world; it was Earth's potential future crystallized in the night sky, now looming larger than ever before.

A Global Awakening

This celestial warning galvanized humanity unlike any previous environmental movement. The abstractions of climate science had suddenly become concrete—visible to anyone who looked upward at dusk. For many, this cosmic perspective finally transformed climate change from a distant, theoretical concern into an immediate, visceral reality.

A new global consensus emerged as nations accelerated carbon-reduction initiatives and invested unprecedented resources in renewable energy development. Reforestation projects expanded across continents, while industrial emission standards tightened dramatically. International cooperation, previously hampered by short-term economic interests, found new momentum in this shared cosmic perspective.

Yet resistance persisted. Certain governments delayed meaningful action, unwilling to sacrifice immediate economic advantages for long-term survival. Industries that had prospered from fossil fuel economies lobbied against systemic reforms, citing economic disruption and national sovereignty.

The debate continued even as evidence of planetary distress mounted—extended droughts, increasingly destructive hurricanes, and catastrophic wildfires grew in frequency and intensity. The scientific data was unequivocal, but the political will to address it remained fragmented.

Venus' orbital stabilization had granted Earth a reprieve from cosmic destruction, but the more insidious threat of self-inflicted climate catastrophe continued to build. The question wasn't whether humans possessed the technological capacity to address climate change—it was whether we could overcome our own psychological and political limitations to implement solutions before crossing irreversible thresholds.

Each evening, Venus hung in our sky as a constant reminder—its brilliant glow nearly twice as large as before, a celestial sentinel watching over Earth. For those who gazed upward, it wasn't merely a beautiful sight; it was simultaneously a warning of potential catastrophe and a promise of what might still be preserved.

We had survived Venus's close encounter. But could we survive our own self-destructive tendencies?

After the Venus Event, people around the world finally got serious about climate change. Citizens took to the streets, demanding real action instead of empty promises. This grassroots pressure led to meaningful agreements that forced governments to protect our environment with stronger regulations. We've seen money pouring into renewable energy research, creating impressive advancements in solar power, wind technology, and even fusion.

Carbon capture projects have gained momentum too, working to pull existing greenhouse gases from our atmosphere. Venus had offered us a second chance, but nobody knew if we'd make good use of it.

Scientists seized this unique opportunity, using Venus's newfound proximity to study it in unprecedented detail. High-resolution images revealed ancient formations shaped by massive volcanic eruptions from its distant past.

These discoveries led researchers to believe that Venus might have experienced its own climate crisis long ago, when volcanic activity released enormous amounts of carbon dioxide, creating the thick blanket of greenhouse gases that now traps its scorching heat. Looking at Venus was like glimpsing a possible future for Earth.

With travel time to Venus significantly reduced, we launched new missions of robotic explorers. These machines pierced through Venus's dense atmosphere, sending back precious information about weather systems, geological activity, and atmospheric makeup. Scientists realized that by understanding Venus more deeply, we could better understand—and perhaps prevent—Earth's potential fate.

The Legacy of the Evening Star

The Venus Event changed more than just science. It transformed our culture completely. Poets, philosophers, and religious thinkers all found new meaning in Venus's transformation. Faith leaders interpreted it as a powerful sign that the universe remains in constant motion and that humanity's story isn't yet finished. Artists captured the strange new skies in their paintings, while musicians created beautiful symphonies celebrating the "Evening Star Reborn." Writers imagined hopeful futures where we learned from Venus's example and chose a different path for Earth.

As years turned into decades, our changed sky became normal. For children born after the Venus Event, that brighter, larger Venus was simply how the night had always been. They didn't see it as something frightening, but as a symbol of how people can come together when facing disaster.

Universities created special Venus research programs, attracting young students who had grown up inspired by both the crisis and our response to it. In many ways, Venus had become humanity's greatest teacher.

But the deepest change happened in how we think about ourselves.

Before Venus came so close, we viewed space with interest but also with a certain smugness. We assumed the cosmos would stay fixed and distant, never touching our daily lives. The Venus Event shattered that comfortable belief. We suddenly understood that the universe is alive and sometimes unpredictable. Earth isn't fighting its battles alone—it's part of a complex, fragile system where everything we do matters.

We started seeing ourselves differently: not just as people living on Earth, but as caretakers responsible for keeping our planet liveable for future generations.

Venus—once worshipped as the goddess of love and beauty—had become something more meaningful. She became our warning, our lesson, and most importantly, our second chance.

And so, Earth continues its journey around the sun, with Venus shining brightly beside us—a guardian light reminding us of what matters most.

Would we listen? Would we learn? Or would we, too, someday mirror the fate of our fiery sister?

Only time would tell.

But now, at least, we were paying attention.

Back to the Beginning

Back in suburban Melbourne, Andy stood again in his backyard— with the same slightly battered telescope, but a different man.

The air was cool. Autumn had returned, and with it, the familiar scents of eucalyptus and damp soil. The Labrador next door barked at something, then lost interest. Everything, somehow, had returned to normal.

Almost.

Andy focused his telescope, dialling it toward Venus's new place in the sky. It wasn't quite where it used to be—just enough off to make him pause, the way a favourite chair might feel strange if moved a few centimetres.

There she was - twice as big and still burning bright. But she no longer stared down at Earth with menace.

Andy smiled, a slow, knowing smile. He reached into his pocket, pulled out a small notepad, and scribbled a single line:

"Venus... settled."

Then he looked up again, eyes reflecting the shimmering planet that had almost destroyed his world—but instead, had merely changed it.

Epilogue II
Consequences for Our Planet Earth

Venus's runaway greenhouse effect isn't just a distant planetary curiosity—it's a clanging alarm bell for Earth. Once a potentially habitable world with oceans like our own, Venus transformed into a hellscape of acid clouds and crushing atmospheric pressure, where surface temperatures can melt lead.

This planetary nightmare scenario unfolded when rising temperatures triggered a vicious cycle: heat released water vapor, water vapor trapped more heat, and carbon dioxide escaped from rocks into the atmosphere, creating a feedback loop that spiralled beyond any point of return. The result? A toxic pressure cooker of a planet that stands as a cosmic warning sign.

For Earth-like planets throughout our galaxy, Venus represents the thin line between paradise and purgatory. Scientists hunting for habitable exoplanets now recognize this "Venus Zone" where promising worlds might actually be death traps in disguise. Even more chilling is the realization that our own blue marble, well within the "Goldilocks Zone" of our solar system, but with its own delicate atmospheric balance, could potentially follow this same catastrophic trajectory.

Venus doesn't whisper warnings—it screams them! Its transformation from Earth's twin to uninhabitable inferno delivers a gut-punching lesson in that climate systems can reach tipping points where collapse becomes unstoppable. As we pump greenhouse gases into our own atmosphere, Venus serves not as a distant scientific curiosity, but as a scorched monument to what happens when planetary climate change spirals beyond control.

Image: NASA

The **Blue Marble** is a famous photograph of the Earth taken on December 7, 1972, by the crew of the Apollo 17 spacecraft en route to the Moon at a distance of 29,400 kilometres (18,300 miles).

Appendices
Venus – A Scientific and Historical Profile

Appendix A: Venus – A Scientific Overview

This section provides a foundational understanding of Venus as a planetary body, its physical characteristics, orbital dynamics, atmospheric conditions, and how it compares to Earth.

Appendix B: Geological Features of Venus

Venus possesses a fascinating and diverse geological landscape. This section explores its mountains, volcanoes, unique formations, and surface deformations observed through radar and satellite mapping.

Appendix C: Soviet Venera and Vega Missions

The Soviet Union led the most extensive series of missions to Venus in the 20th century. This section details the pioneering Venera program and the ambitious dual-flyby Vega missions.

Appendix D: U.S. and European Missions

NASA and ESA contributed significantly to our understanding of Venus through a combination of flybys, orbiters, and radar imaging missions. This section summarizes the major Western missions and their key findings.

Appendix E: Future Missions and Renewed Interest

Interest in Venus exploration has been revitalized in recent years, driven by new technology and unanswered questions. This section outlines upcoming missions and what they hope to discover.

Appendix F: Venus Habitability Concepts

Despite its harsh surface conditions, Venus presents intriguing opportunities for high-atmosphere habitation. This section explores scientific proposals for floating cities, comparative habitability, and long-term colonization concepts.

Appendix G: Scientific Foundations

Explores the real-world astronomical research behind planetary orbital instability, including simulations by Jacques Laskar showing that rare but possible gravitational disturbances—particularly involving Mercury—could lead to chaotic changes in neighbouring planetary orbits.

Appendix H: Image Credits and Attributions

Images featured throughout this book, particularly those relating to the Soviet Venera and Vega missions, are sourced from a range of public and archival collections.

Appendix A
Venus - A Scientific Profile

Introduction: Meeting Our Nearest Neighbour

This section provides a foundational understanding of Venus as a planetary body, its physical characteristics, orbital dynamics, atmospheric conditions, and how it compares to Earth.

Image: NASA/JPL

Let's take a journey to explore Earth's closest planetary neighbor, Venus. Named after the Roman goddess of love and beauty, this fascinating world holds many secrets and surprises that might just change how you think about our solar system.

Size and Structure

- Almost Earth's Twin: Venus is remarkably similar in size to Earth, with a diameter of 12,104 kilometers—just 650 kilometers smaller than our home planet. That's like comparing a basketball to another basketball that's only about 5% smaller!

- Mass Matters: Venus weighs in at about 80% of Earth's mass, making it our closest planetary match in the solar system. This similarity in mass means that:

  ➤ The internal structure is likely very similar to Earth's

  ➤ It has a similar layered composition with a core, mantle, and crust

  ➤ The gravity is about 90% of Earth's; you'd feel slightly lighter, but not by much

- **Core Facts: Scientists believe Venus has:**

  ➤ Dense iron core approximately 3,000 kilometers in radius.

  ➤ A molten rocky mantle making up much of the planet, although unlike Earth, Venus does not possess tectonic plates. Therefore, its thin crust is being constantly reshaped by volcanic activity.

- **Surface Features and Composition:**

  ➤ Mostly covered in flat lands, with six major mountainous regions.

  ➤ At least 85% of the surface is covered by volcanic flows.

  ➤ Features active volcanoes, including Maat Mons, which rises up to 8 kilometres high.

  ➤ Surface was extensively mapped by the Magellan missions (1990-1994).

Proximity and Orbit

- **Closest planetary neighbor:** When Venus and Earth align at their nearest point, they're only 38 million kilometers apart. To put this in perspective:

  ➤ Mars at its closest is 56 million kilometers away

  ➤ Mercury averages 91 million kilometers

  ➤ Jupiter is a distant 628 million kilometers

- ➢ Saturn is 1.2 billion kilometers away
- ➢ Uranus sits at 2.6 billion kilometers
- ➢ Neptune is 4.3 billion kilometers from Earth

- **Orbital Peculiarities:**
  - ➢ Venus has an almost perfect circular orbit around the Sun
  - ➢ It completes one orbit every 225 Earth days
  - ➢ The planet maintains a remarkably stable distance from the Sun at about 108 million kilometers
  - ➢ Unlike other planets' elliptical orbits, Venus's circular path is unique in our solar system

Rotation and Day Length

- **The Backward Planet:** Venus rotates in the opposite direction to most planets, meaning:
  - ➢ The Sun rises in the west and sets in the east
  - ➢ This retrograde rotation might be the result of a massive collision in the planet's early history
  - ➢ It's one of only two planets with this backwards rotation (Uranus is the other)

- **The Long Day:**
  - ➢ One Venusian day lasts 243 Earth days
  - ➢ This is longer than Venus's year (225 Earth days)
  - ➢ It's the longest day of any planet in our solar system
  - ➢ This means that if you lived on Venus, you'd celebrate your birthday before you'd see a single sunrise!

Surface Conditions

- **Extreme Temperature:**
  - ➢ Surface temperature averages 475°C (887°F)

- Hot enough to melt lead, zinc, and many other metals
- Hotter than Mercury despite being further from the Sun
- Temperature remains fairly constant due to the thick atmosphere
- No seasonal variations like we have on Earth

- **Crushing Pressure:**
  - Atmospheric pressure is 90 times greater than Earth's sea level
  - Equivalent to the pressure 1,000 meters deep in Earth's oceans
  - Would instantly crush unprotected spacecraft or humans
  - Requires specially designed equipment for exploration

- **Volcanic Landscape:**
  - Over 1,600 major volcanoes identified
  - Many volcanoes are over 100 kilometers across
  - Volcanic plains cover about 80% of the surface
  - Most volcanoes are believed to be dormant, but some might still be active
  - Volcanic activity might contribute to the thick atmosphere

Atmosphere and Weather

- **Thick Atmospheric Soup:**
  - 96.5% carbon dioxide
  - Creates the most severe greenhouse effect in our solar system
  - Traps heat incredibly efficiently
  - Contains layers of sulfuric acid clouds
  - Almost completely blocks view of the surface from space

- **Extreme Weather:**
  - Wind speeds reach up to 724 kilometers per hour
  - Faster than the strongest tornadoes on Earth

➤ Lightning may be caused by volcanic ash rather than rain

➤ No rainfall as we know it - too hot for liquid water

➤ Constant acid rain that evaporates before reaching the surface

Visibility from Earth

- **The Brightest Natural Object (after the Sun and Moon):**

  ➤ Often mistaken for a UFO due to its brightness

  ➤ Visible in daylight if you know where to look

  ➤ Goes through phases like the Moon

  ➤ Can cast shadows on Earth on moonless nights

  ➤ Has been misidentified as an aircraft by pilots

- **Historical Observations:**

  ➤ Tracked by Babylonians as far back as 1600 BCE

  ➤ First planet to have its phases observed by telescope (Galileo, 1610)

  ➤ The first planet humans sent a spacecraft to (Mariner 2, 1962)

  ➤ One of only two planets that can transit the Sun as seen from Earth

  ➤ Has been worshipped by many ancient cultures

Impact Craters and Surface Features

- **Preserved History:**

  ➤ Over 1,000 impact craters identified

  ➤ Most craters remain in pristine condition

  ➤ No erosion from water or weather

  ➤ Youngest craters still have radiating debris patterns

  ➤ Provides insights into the planet's geological history

- **Unique Surface Features:**
  - ➢ Vast plains of volcanic rock
  - ➢ Mountain ranges higher than Earth's Everest
  - ➢ Deep canyons and valleys
  - ➢ Evidence of ancient lava flows
  - ➢ Possible recent volcanic activity

Future Exploration Potential

- **Atmospheric Habitation Possibilities:**
  - ➢ 50 kilometers above the surface, conditions are surprisingly Earth-like
  - ➢ Temperature range: 0-50°C
  - ➢ Earth-like atmospheric pressure
  - ➢ Better radiation protection than Mars
  - ➢ Gravity similar to Earth's

- **Past Potential for Life:**
  - ➢ May have had liquid water oceans
  - ➢ Possible habitable conditions 2.9 billion years ago
  - ➢ Could have supported life before Earth
  - ➢ Might hold clues about Earth's future
  - ➢ Current focus of several planned space missions

Appendix B
Geological Features of Venus

Venus possesses a fascinating and diverse geological landscape. This section explores its mountains, volcanoes, unique formations, and surface deformations observed through radar and satellite mapping.

The Six Mountainous Regions of Venus And Selected Volcanoes

1. **Maxwell Montes** – The tallest mountain range on Venus, located in Ishtar Terra in the northern hemisphere. Peaks reach up to 11 kilometres (higher than Mount Everest).

This radar-generated (CGI) image shows **Maxwell Montes**. The bright feature near the center is the mountain range, and you can see **Cleopatra crater** (a dark circle) nearby.

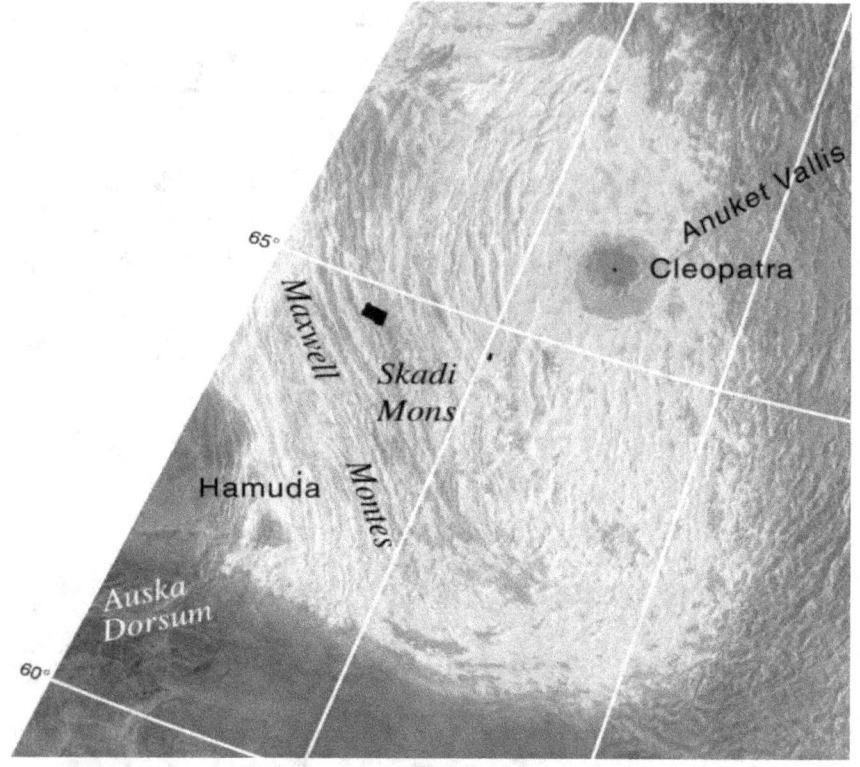

Image: NASA

A map-schematic image of Maxwell Montes in relation to nearby geological features.

2. **Akna Montes** – A mountain range located along the western edge of Lakshmi Planum in Ishtar Terra, characterized by large ridges.

3. **Freya Montes** – Found in Ishtar Terra near the northern highlands, south of Maxwell Montes.

4. **Danu Montes** – Located in the eastern portion of Ishtar Terra.

5. **Ovda Regio** – While more of a highland plateau, it contains mountainous terrain and is often associated with Venusian highlands.

6. **Thetis Regio** – Similar to Ovda, it's a highland region with rugged, mountainous features.

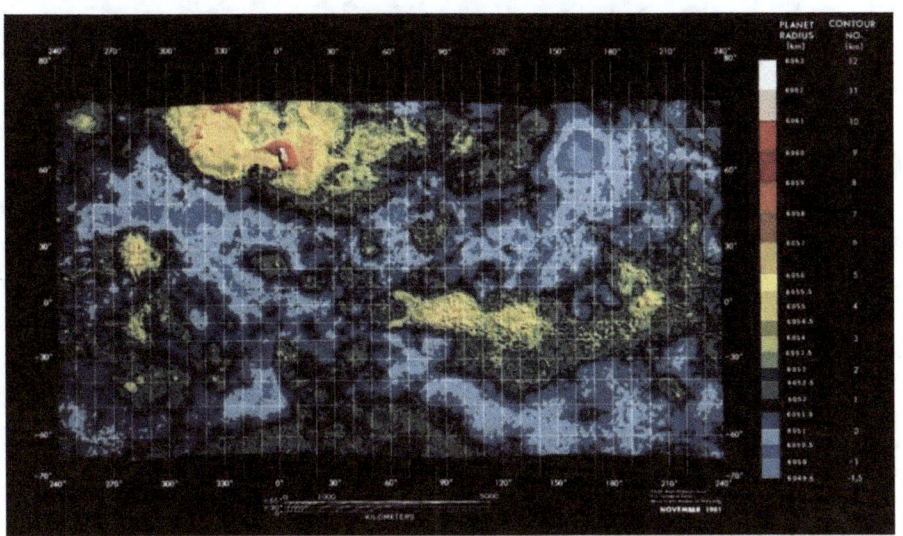

Image:NASA

A map of Venus compiled from data recorded by NASA's Pioneer Venus Orbiter spacecraft beginning in 1978.

Color-coded elevation map, showing the elevated "terrae" or continents in yellow. Ishtar Terra with Maxwell Montes is at the top.

Venus Topographical Map

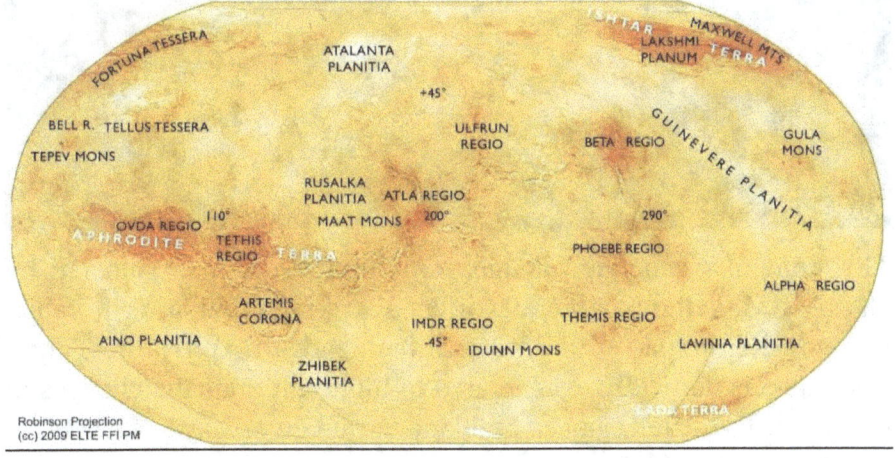

A simplified computer-generated schematic of the previous image outlining the six mountainous regions of Venus. The image is a stylised, topographic visualisation—meaning:

- Locations of the regions are approximately accurate relative to each other.

- Elevations are based on real radar data (from NASA's Magellan mission), often exaggerated slightly to make terrain features more visible.

- The scale (in terms of exact distances or land area) is not precise, and the sizes of features are visually adjusted for clarity.

So, it's not true to scale, but it's a useful and realistic representation of the relative positions and general terrain of those six mountainous regions.

<u>Venus Rift Valleys</u>

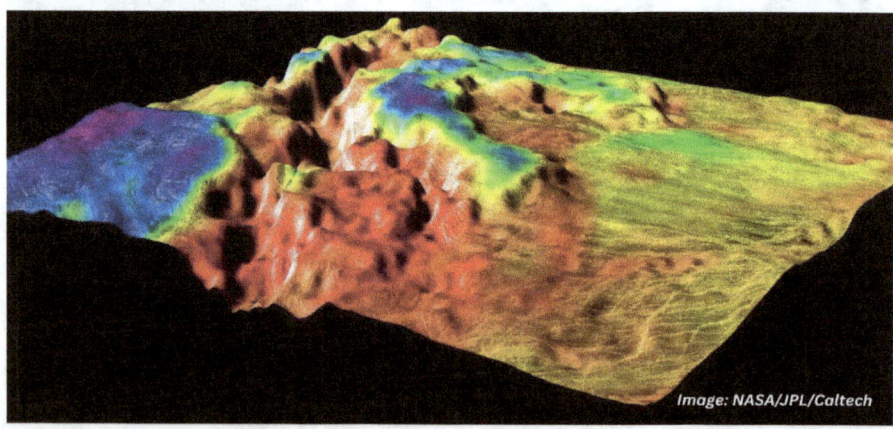

Image: NASA/JPL/Caltech

This computer-generated image, built from radar data gathered by NASA's **Magellan** spacecraft, offers a striking view of a rift valley in **Ovda Regio**, part of the western highlands of **Aphrodite Terra**. The scene is vertically exaggerated to highlight dramatic changes in elevation. To the left, rugged highland terrain gives way to a smoother lava plain on the right—evidence of Venus's powerful geological forces at work.

The colours overlaid on the terrain represent emissivity—how much natural radio and infrared energy the surface emits. These values hint at the composition of the rocks: red areas show higher emissivity, while violet marks the lowest.

Rift valleys like this one are among the most awe-inspiring tectonic features on Venus. They often stretch across elevated regions such as **Beta Regio**, where the crust appears to have bulged upward from deep below. As the surface split apart, enormous rifts formed, crisscrossed with countless fractures and faults. These valleys typically sink 1 to 2 kilometres below the surrounding landscape.

In many ways, Venus's rift valleys resemble geological features found on Earth—like the East African Rift—or even on Mars, such as **Valles Marineris**. All show signs of past volcanic activity. Yet Venus stands apart: without water or wind erosion, its rift valleys remain eerily preserved, like scars frozen in time.

Baltis Vallis is a sinuous channel on Venus ranging from 1 to 3 kilometres wide and about 6,800 kilometres long, slightly longer than the Nile and the **longest known channel of any kind in the Solar System**. What makes Baltis Vallis particularly remarkable is not just its extreme length, but the fact that it maintains a relatively consistent channel structure throughout its course. This suggests that whatever formed it (most likely lava) flowed continuously for an extremely long time without significant interruption, which tells us important information about Venus's past volcanic activity.

Venus Volcanoes

Venus is the most volcanically active planet in the solar system in terms of the sheer number of volcanic features. Its surface is dominated by volcanic landforms, with over 1,600 known volcanoes—though many more likely exist, too small to be detected with current imaging technology. While most of these volcanoes are thought to be dormant, there is evidence that some may still be active today.

Volcanism has played a central role in shaping Venus's surface. Approximately 90% of the surface is composed of basaltic rock, and about 65% consists of vast volcanic plains, forming a patchwork-like mosaic. These features suggest periodic resurfacing events, possibly from extensive lava flows. One major global resurfacing episode is believed to have occurred roughly 500 million years ago, based on the relatively low number and uniform distribution of impact craters.

Among the many volcanic structures on Venus are unusual formations not found on Earth, such as **pancake domes**—broad, flat volcanic domes up to 15 km (9.3 mi) in diameter but less than 1 kilometre (0.62 miles) in height, making them about 100 times larger than similar lava domes on Earth. Venus also hosts other unique features sometimes described as "tick-like" structures, further highlighting the distinctiveness of its volcanic geology.

Quetzalpetlatl Corona

Image: NASA/JPL-Caltech/Peter Rubin

This rather dramatic artist's illustration of the large **Quetzalpetlatl Corona** located in Venus' southern hemisphere depicts active volcanism and a subduction zone, where the foreground crust plunges into the planet's interior.

Maat Mons

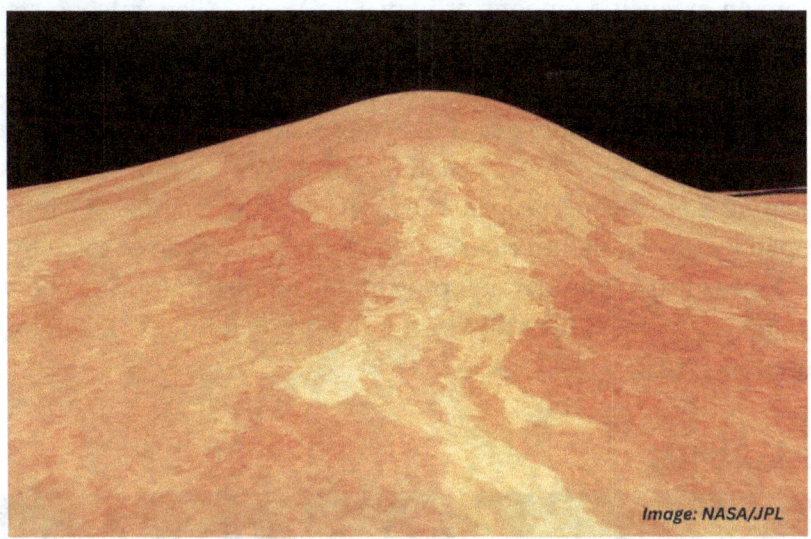

Image: NASA/JPL

Maat Mons pictured in this computer-generated three-dimensional perspective, is the largest volcano on Venus, rising to 8 kilometres (5 miles) above the surface. **Maat Mons** is named after the Egyptian goddess of truth and justice. The simulated hues are based on colour images recorded by the Soviet Venera 13 and 14 lander probes. Lava flows extend for hundreds of kilometers across the fractured plains shown in the foreground, from the base of **Maat Mons**.

Indunn Mons

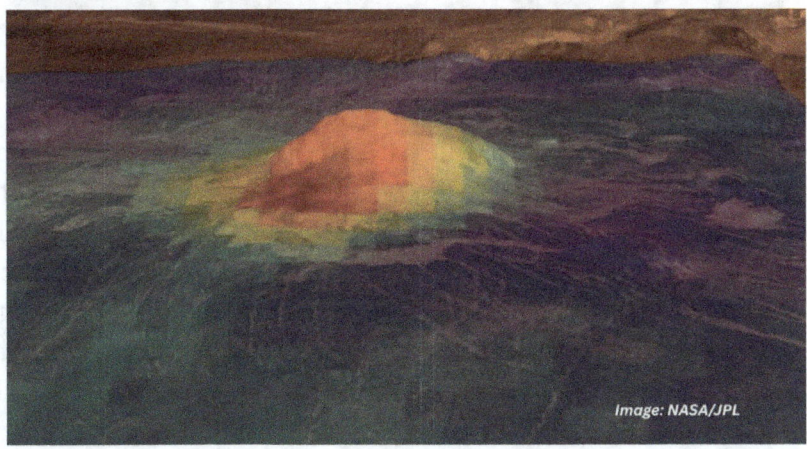

Image: NASA/JPL

Idunn Mons is a prominent volcano located in the **Imdr Regio** region, an extensive igneous province on Venus. The volcano stands about 2.5 km (1.6 mi) above the surrounding terrain and rises approximately 3.6 km above Venus's mean planetary radius. It spans roughly 250 km in diameter. Lava flows from **Idunn Mons** extend outward in all directions, reaching distances of up to 550 km, indicating significant volcanic activity in the region. Originally mapped by the **Magellan** mission, the image shows an overlay by the later **Venus Express** radar mapping, in the reddish colouring showing volcanic activity and lava flows after the original images taken by the **Magellan** craft.

Sapas Mons

Image: NASA/JPL

Lava flows extending from the shield volcano **Sapas Mons** on Venus, in an oblique computer-generated view based on radar data from the Magellan spacecraft. Located in **Alta Regio** in the northeastern part of **Aphrodite Terra, Sapas Mons** is 400 km (250 miles) wide at its base and peaks at 4.5 km (2.8 miles) above Venus's mean radius. The relative brightness of the lava flows in the radar image indicates a rougher surface than that of the surrounding plains. In the distance directly behind **Sapas** rises **Maat Mons**. The image is exaggerated 10 times in the vertical direction to bring out topographic detail. It's simulated colour is based on Soviet **Venera** lander images.

Appendix C
Venera and Vega Missions to Venus

The Soviet Union led the most extensive series of missions to Venus in the 20th century. This section details the pioneering **Venera** program and the ambitious dual-flyby **Vega** missions.

Artist's Impression of Venera 9 on the surface of Venus

Venera 13 and 14 ejected their camera lens covers after landing—see above and below.

Images: Courtesy RSA

The **Venera** landers survived on Venus' surface from just 23 minutes (**Venera 7**) to 127 minutes (**Venera 13**) before succumbing to the intense heat and pressure—essentially, they baked until they failed.

Replica of **Venera 9** lander on display at the K. E. Tsiolkovsky Museum of the History of Cosmonautics, Kaluga, Russia.

Table of Venera Missions to Venus

Mission	Year	Key Outcomes
Venera 1	1961	First Soviet attempt at a Venus flyby; lost contact before reaching the planet.
Venera 2	1965	Flyby mission; contact lost before data transmission.
Venera 3	1965	First spacecraft to impact another planet (Venus); failed before sending data.
Venera 4	1967	First probe to transmit data from Venus' atmosphere; confirmed CO_2-rich environment.
Venera 5	1969	Atmospheric probe; improved measurements of Venus' pressure and composition.
Venera 6	1969	Similar to Venera 5; confirmed Venus' extreme atmospheric conditions.
Venera 7	1970	**First successful landing on another planet**; transmitted 23 minutes of surface data.
Venera 8	1972	Improved surface data collection; confirmed Venus' high temperatures and pressure.
Venera 9	1975	**First image from the surface of Venus (black & white)**; confirmed rocky terrain.
Venera 10	1975	Another successful landing; transmitted surface panoramas.
Venera 11	1978	Landed but failed to return images due to lens cap issue; detected lightning.
Venera 12	1978	Similar to Venera 11; recorded powerful lightning activity.
Venera 13	1981	**First color images from Venus**; confirmed basaltic rock composition.
Venera 14	1981	Successful imaging; **lens cap landed under soil probe, rendering experiment useless.**
Venera 15	1983	Orbiter mission; **mapped Venus' surface using radar** (first high-resolution radar mapping).
Venera 16	1983	Orbiter mission; continued radar mapping, refining Venus' topography.

Historical and Scientific Significance

What makes the Venera program particularly remarkable is that more than four decades later, these Soviet missions remain our only direct contact with the Venusian surface. No other nation has successfully landed functioning spacecraft on Venus. The images and data they returned represent humanity's only ground-truth information about the surface of our nearest planetary neighbour.

The program's achievements are especially impressive considering they were accomplished with 1970s-80s computing technology, during the Cold War, and with computing power far less sophisticated than today's smartphones.

The Venera program was groundbreaking, providing humanity with its first direct observations of Venus's harsh environment and confirming that its surface conditions were far more extreme than originally imagined. In fact, as previously noted, early Soviet expectations pictured Venus as Earth-like—featuring oceans, mountains, lush vegetation, and even exotic life. This belief was so strong that Venera 1 was equipped with a buoyant capsule, complete with a Soviet (USSR) pendant, intended to float on what was presumed to be a Venusian ocean!

The Soviet Venera program has never received it's due recognition. These missions gave us our first-ever glimpses of Venus's surface—an incredible human achievement that got overshadowed by Cold War politics and limited media coverage in the West. The Venera spacecraft had to survive conditions that would destroy most technology in minutes, yet they managed to land, take pictures, and send back crucial data. Their accomplishments still form the foundation of our Venus knowledge today.

Front and rear surface photographs taken by Venera 13 & 14

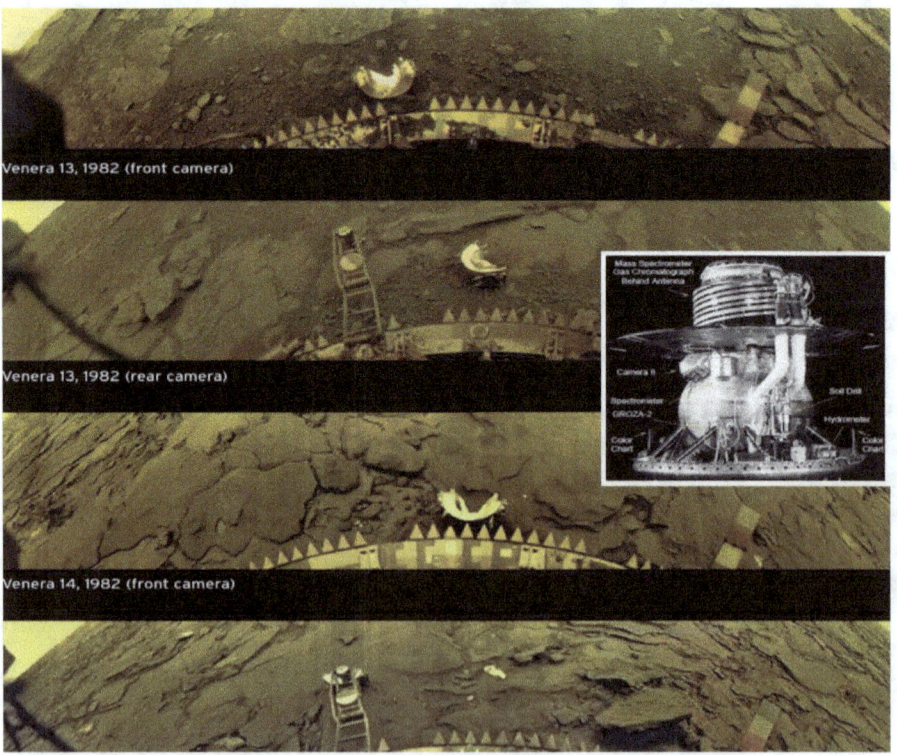

ВЕНЕРА-14   ОБРАБОТКА ИППИ АН СССР И ЦДКС

ВЕНЕРА-14   ОБРАБОТКА ИППИ АН СССР И ЦДКС

Images: Russian Academy of Sciences & Fred Stryk

Vega 1 and 2 Missions

The **Vega** program (Russian: Вега) was a series of Soviet Venus missions that also took advantage of the appearance of comet Halley's Comet in 1986. **Vega 1** and **Vega 2** were uncrewed spacecraft. They had a two-part mission to investigate Venus and also flyby Halley's Comet.

These spacecraft were designated **VeGa**, a contraction of *Venera* and *Gallei* (Венера and Галлей respectively, the Russian words for "Venus" and "Halley"). The spacecraft design was based on the previous **Venera 9** and **Venera 10** missions.

The two spacecraft were launched on 15 and 21 December 1984, respectively.

Vega 1 and 2 both included Venus lander components that successfully touched down on the surface of Venus on June 11 and 15, 1985, respectively.

The **Vega** craft included:

1. A Venus lander that descended to the surface
2. A balloon that was deployed in Venus's atmosphere
3. A flyby spacecraft that continued on to observe Halley's Comet

121

Like their **Venera** predecessors, the **Vega** landers could only function for a short time in the extreme Venusian environment before being destroyed by the heat and pressure.

So, while the **Vega** missions are sometimes discussed separately because their primary goal was Halley's Comet, they did indeed add to the Soviet Union's achievements as the only nation to successfully land functioning probes on Venus's surface.

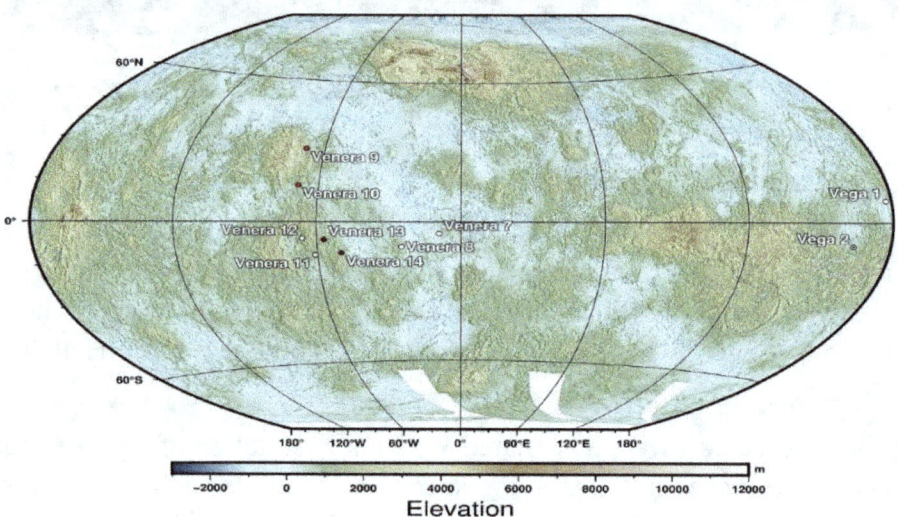

Map of Vega and Venera landing sites on Venus. Red points denote sites returning images from the surface, based on mapping from Pioneer Venus Orbiter, Magellan, and Venera 15 and 16.

Appendix D
US, European And Japanese Missions

NASA and ESA contributed significantly to our understanding of Venus through a combination of flybys, orbiters, and radar imaging missions. This section summarizes the major Western missions and their key findings.

Mariner

NASA's Mariner 2, 5 & 10 missions to Venus (1962–1974) achieved the first successful planetary flybys, revealing Venus's extreme surface temperatures, dense atmosphere, and pervasive cloud cover. These early missions laid the foundation for future exploration.

Mariner 2 (1962)

Image: NASA/JPL

Mariner 5 (1967)

Image: NASA/JPL

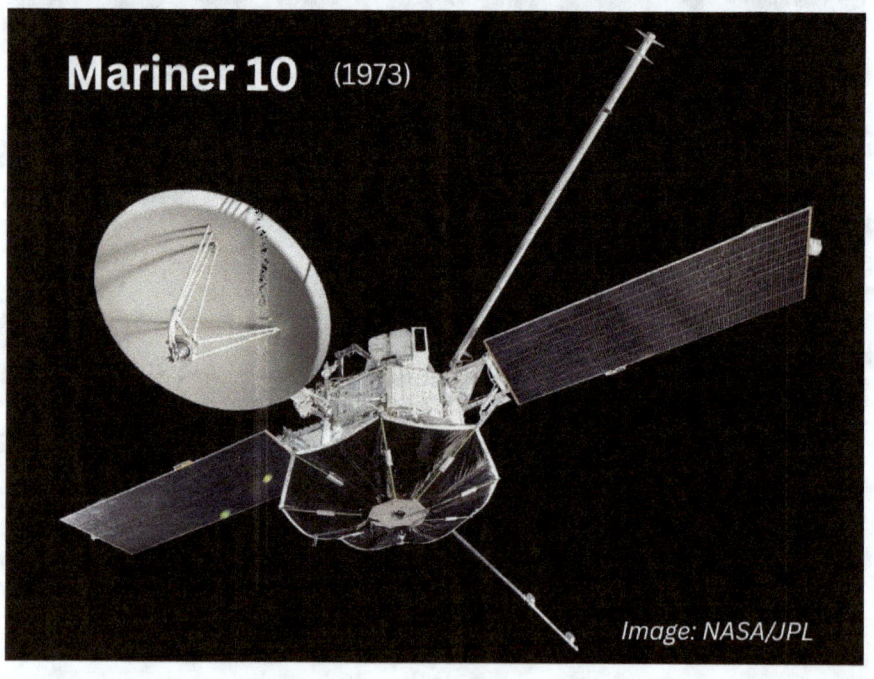

Mariner 10 (1973)

Image: NASA/JPL

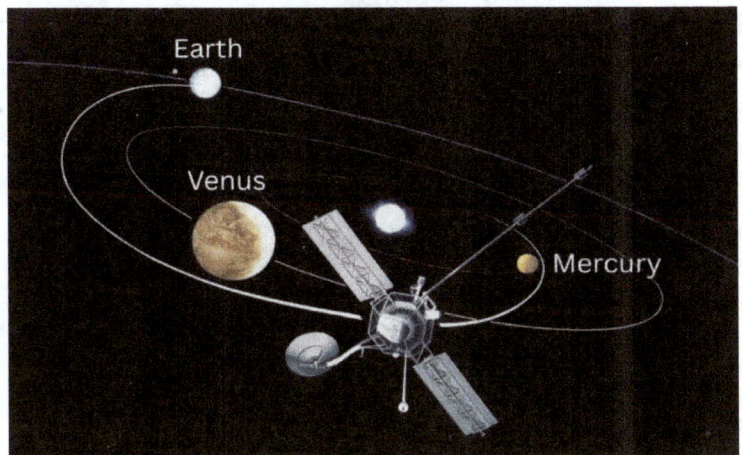

An artist's impression of the Mariner 10 mission, as it used a flyby of the planet Venus to allow the spacecraft to rendezvous with Mercury.   *Image: NASA/JPL*

Pioneer Venus

NASA's Pioneer Venus missions in 1978 revolutionized our understanding of Venus, with **Pioneer Venus 1** (also called **Pioneer 12**) creating the first radar map of the planet's surface during its remarkable 14-year orbital mission, staying in orbit throughout the 1980's and into the early 1990's.

Artist's impression of Pioneer 1 in orbit above Venus

Image: NASA/JPL

Pioneer Venus 2 (also known as **Pioneer Venus Multiprobe**, or **Pioneer 13**), was a spacecraft also launched in 1978, deployed four atmospheric probes that provided unprecedented data on Venus's atmospheric composition, temperature, and pressure.

Pioneer 2

Artist's impression of Pioneer 2 approaching Venus

Image: NASA/JPL

Together, these **Pioneer** missions marked a turning point in the scientific understanding of Venus, in revealing Venus's mountainous terrain, complex cloud structures, and harsh surface conditions, and establishing fundamental knowledge that has informed all subsequent exploration of our nearest planetary neighbour.

Magellan

The **Magellan** probe was the first interplanetary mission to be launched from the Space Shuttle, in this case Atlantis. Launched on May 4, 1989, **Magellan** used radar mapping to penetrate Venus's thick clouds, producing the first high-resolution global maps of the surface. It revealed vast volcanic plains, mountain ranges, and evidence of tectonic deformation, transforming our understanding of Venusian geology.

Magellan in a deployment position in Atlantis' payload bay

An artist's impression of Magellan radar-mapping the surface of Venus.

The **Pioneer**, **Mariner**, and **Magellan** missions collectively transformed our understanding of Venus from a mysterious cloud-shrouded world to a well-mapped planet with known surface features, atmospheric composition, and extreme conditions, establishing it as a crucial comparative case study for planetary evolution and climate change.

European Space Agency (ESA): Venus Express

Venus Express was the European Space Agency's (ESA) first mission dedicated to exploring Venus, launched in November 2005 and arriving at the planet in April 2006. The spacecraft entered a polar orbit and began a long-term scientific study, sending back continuous data until November 2014.

The main goal of **Venus Express** was to conduct an in-depth investigation of Venus's atmosphere, especially its structure, composition, and dynamics, as well as its plasma environment and the way the upper atmosphere interacts with the solar wind. The mission also examined the greenhouse effect, surface features, and surface-atmosphere interactions.

One of its key findings was that Venus has lost a significant amount of water to space over billions of years.

Venus Express also detected a sudden rise and fall in sulphur dioxide levels in the upper atmosphere shortly after arriving. This observation suggests the possibility of recent volcanic activity, possibly caused by large eruptions releasing volcanic gases into the atmosphere.

The spacecraft carried seven scientific instruments, enabling the first long-duration atmospheric study of Venus—something previous missions had not achieved. These extended observations were crucial to improving our understanding of Venus's complex climate system.

Contact with **Venus Express** was lost on 28 November 2014, and **ESA** officially ended the mission shortly after, on 16 December 2014.

Artists' impressions of Venus Express in orbit around Venus - *ESA*

Japan Aerospace Exploration Agency (JAXA): Akatsuki (Venus Climate Orbiter)

Akatsuki (あかつき, meaning "Dawn") was **Japan's** first successful mission to explore another planet. Also known as the Venus Climate Orbiter (VCO) or Planet-C, the spacecraft was launched aboard an H-IIA rocket on May 20, 2010, by the **Japan Aerospace Exploration Agency (JAXA)**.

Although its initial attempt to enter Venusian orbit on December 6, 2010, failed, **Akatsuki** remained operational and orbited the Sun for five years. On December 7, 2015, JAXA engineers successfully placed the probe into an alternative elliptical orbit around Venus.

The primary objective of **Akatsuki** was to study Venus's atmosphere—focusing on weather patterns, cloud dynamics, and the search for signs of active volcanism. Among its most significant discoveries was a giant stationary atmospheric wave, along with detailed observations of atmospheric circulation.

The mission far exceeded expectations. Designed for a 4.5-year lifespan, **Akatsuki** continued to deliver scientific data for nearly 14 years. However, in April 2024, **JAXA** lost contact with the spacecraft, and despite recovery efforts, communications could not be reestablished—marking the official end of the mission.

Images Courtesy of ISAS/JAXA.

Artist's impression of **Akatsuki** traveling forward to enter orbit around Venus.

Artist's impression of **Akatsuki** insertion into orbit around Venus, on the 7 December 2015.

Summary of Venus Missions by Country and Outcome

Country/Agency	Total Missions	% of All Missions	Successful Missions	% Success (Country)	% Success (Overall)	Failed Missions	% Failure (Country)	% Failure (Overall)
Soviet/Russian	31	56.4%	16	51.6%	29.1%	15	48.4%	27.3%
US/NASA	17	30.9%	9	52.9%	16.4%	8	47.1%	14.5%
ESA	4	7.3%	2	50.0%	3.6%	2	50.0%	3.6%
Japan	3	5.5%	0	0.0%	0.0%	3	100.0%	5.5%
Total	**55**	**100.0%**	**27**	**49.1%**	**49.1%**	**28**	**50.9%**	**50.9%**

Although the preceding appendices are detailed, they do not provide an exhaustive list of all Venus mission attempts—particularly the many failed or partially successful ones (or Venus fly-bys)—in humanity's ongoing quest to explore our closest planetary neighbour. Most of the failures occurred during the early years of the 1960s and 1970s, when technological limitations were unable to overcome the immense challenges posed by both the complex engineering demands and the planet's extremely hostile environment.

A truly comprehensive and analytical account of every attempt would require an entirely separate volume!

To the best of my knowledge and research, the table above summarizes a total of 55 missions to Venus (E&OE) conducted over roughly 60 years, from the 1960s through the 2010s, by various nations. Of these, the overall success rate hovers around 50%, which likely reflects the high number of early failures. Another contributing factor is that, over time, Venus has declined in priority for interplanetary exploration among most—if not all—spacefaring nations. (See the chart below regarding NASA expenditures, which likely reflects the broader trend across major space agencies.)

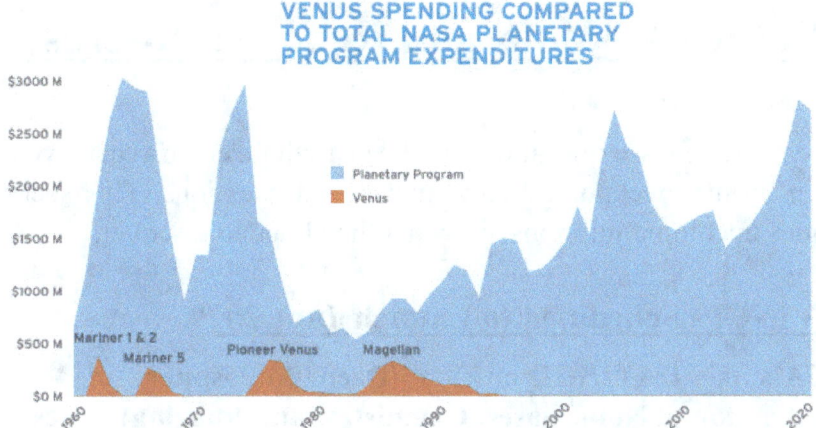

VENUS SPENDING COMPARED TO TOTAL NASA PLANETARY PROGRAM EXPENDITURES

Courtesy of The Planetary Society 2021

The chart above shows the gap between NASA's expenditure on Venus' exploration, in comparison to it's total planetary program budget. NASA has spent approximately $US3.65 billion on dedicated Venus missions out of roughly $US97 billion spent on it's robotic planetary program (2019 figures).

Appendix E
Future Missions and Renewed Interest

Interest in Venus exploration has been revitalized in recent years, driven by new technology and unanswered questions. This section outlines upcoming missions and what they hope to discover.

DAVINCI - Scheduled to Launch June 2029

NASA's the **DAVINCI** mission **(Deep Atmosphere of Venus Investigation of Noble gases, Chemistry, and Imaging)** represents humanity's ambitious return to Venus, combining both a flyby spacecraft and an atmospheric descent probe to unlock the secrets of our planetary neighbour. **DAVINCI** is tentatively scheduled to launch June 2029 and enter the Venusian atmosphere in June 2031. **DAVINCI** will be the first mission to visit the Venusian atmosphere since 1984. This pioneering endeavour seeks to address fundamental questions about Venus's puzzling evolutionary path.

At its core, **DAVINCI** aims to measure isotopes and trace gases in Venus's lower atmosphere, with particular attention to sulphur compounds that could reveal current volcanic activity. The mission will also analyse noble gases like helium and xenon—elemental time capsules that preserve crucial information about Venus's ancient history and its past water inventory. By comparing the noble gas composition of Venus with that of Earth and Mars, scientists hope to unravel why these three worlds, despite their similar origins, evolved along such dramatically different trajectories.

Images: NASA

The mission's comprehensive science objectives extend beyond atmospheric chemistry to understand the origin and evolution of Venus's atmosphere, explore the possibilities of an early Venusian ocean, determine the rate of volcanic activity, and investigate the nature, origin, and history of the tesserae—Venus's unique geological features. Through **DAVINCI**, we stand at the threshold of answering one of planetary science's most compelling questions: how and why did Venus, Earth's sister planet in size and composition, become so fundamentally different from our habitable world?

135

During its 63-minute descent, **DAVINCI** will collect and return measurements of Venus' atmospheric composition.

VERITAS - Scheduled to Launch June 2031

As part of **NASA's Discovery Program**, VERITAS (**Venus Emissivity, Radio Science, InSAR, Topography, and Spectroscopy**) is an upcoming mission from **NASA's Jet Propulsion Laboratory (JPL)** to map the surface of the planet Venus in high resolution. The combination of topography, near-infrared spectroscopy, and radar image data will provide knowledge of Venus's tectonic and impact history, gravity, geochemistry, the timing and mechanisms of volcanic resurfacing, and the mantle processes responsible for them.

Artist's impression of **VERITAS** at Venus

Image: NASA/JPL-Caltech

EnVision - Scheduled to Launch December 2031

The **European Space Agency (ESA) i**n collaboration with **NASA**, is developing **EnVision** as an orbital mission to Venus, that is designed to perform high-resolution radar mapping and atmospheric studies. **EnVision** aims to help scientists understand the relationships between Venus' geological activity and it's atmosphere, and to investigate why Venus and Earth took such different evolutionary paths.

Artist's impression of **EnVision** at Venus

Image: ESA/Paris Observatory/VR2Planets & NASA/JPL-Caltech

Venera D - Scheduled to Launch in 2031

Roscosmos's Venera-D (short for *"Dolgozhivushchaya"*, meaning "long-lasting" in Russian) is a proposed Russian mission to Venus, currently slated for launch no earlier than 2031, aligning with an optimal planetary transfer window. The mission is expected to include both an orbiter and a lander, making it Russia's first independent Venus exploration effort since the Soviet era.

As the spiritual successor to the historic Venera program, **Venera-D** would mark the first Russian-built Venus probe since the dissolution of the Soviet Union. It is envisioned as the flagship of a new generation of Russian planetary missions. A key goal of the mission is to deliver a surface lander that can endure Venus's extreme conditions for at least three hours—surpassing the current record of 127 minutes set by Venera 13 in 1982.

Accompanying the lander, the **Venera-D orbiter** is expected to operate for at least three years, providing high-resolution radar mapping, atmospheric studies, and potential data relay support. The lander itself, built on heritage Venera designs, would carry instruments to study surface composition, seismology, and meteorology, enduring crushing pressure and searing heat that have foiled all other landers within hours.

Artist's impression of **Venera-D** approaching Venus

Image: RussianSpaceWeb.com

Venus Life Finder - Scheduled to Launch 2026

Venus Life Finder is a privately funded atmospheric mission developed by **Rocket Lab** in collaboration with the **Massachusetts Institute of Technology (MIT).** Now scheduled for launch no earlier than 2026, the mission will deploy a small atmospheric probe using **Rocket Lab's Photon Explorer** spacecraft.

Its primary goal is to search for organic molecules—including **phosphine**, a potential biosignature—within Venus's upper cloud layers. The probe will carry a single instrument, an auto fluorescing nephelometer, designed to analyse cloud particles for chemical signs of life.

This mission is part of the broader **Morning Star** program and may become the first privately-led mission to another planet. Interest in Venusian astrobiology intensified following a 2020 announcement that trace amounts of phosphine—on Earth associated with microbial life—had been detected in Venus's clouds, where temperatures and pressures are similar to those on Earth.

Shukrayaan-1: India's First Venus Mission - Scheduled to Launch in 2028

The Indian Space Research Organisation (ISRO) is set to launch **Shukrayaan-1**, its first mission to Venus, on March 29, 2028, with orbital arrival expected by July 19, 2028. The mission will deploy an orbiter to study Venus's atmosphere, ionosphere, surface geology, and magnetic field.

Equipped with a synthetic aperture radar, infrared and ultraviolet sensors, and instruments for ionospheric analysis, **Shukrayaan-1** aims to investigate the planet's thick cloud layers, primarily composed of carbon dioxide and sulfuric acid, and search for signs of geological and volcanic activity.

While not a dedicated astrobiology mission, the data may also support ongoing speculation about the possibility of microbial life in Venus's upper atmosphere—where conditions are more Earth-like.

Shukrayaan-1 marks a significant step in India's planetary exploration efforts and may help unlock some of Venus's long-standing mysteries.

Image: The Indian Space Research Organisation (ISRO)

Appendix F
Venus Habitability Concepts

Despite its harsh surface conditions, Venus presents intriguing opportunities for high-atmosphere habitation. This section explores scientific proposals for floating cities, comparative habitability, and long-term colonization concepts.

Possible Future Human Habitation at High Altitude

➢ One of the most compelling arguments for exploring human habitation near Venus lies in the surprising habitability of its upper atmosphere. At an altitude of 50 to 55 kilometres above the surface, Venus offers a zone of remarkable hospitality. Here, temperatures range from 20 to 37°C, atmospheric pressure closely mirrors that of Earth's sea level, and gravity pulls at about **0.9 g**, or 91% of Earth's gravity (9.81 m/s²). This last point is especially significant: unlike Mars, whose surface gravity is only **0.38 g** (3.71 m/s²), or about one third of Earth's gravity, Venus' Near-Earth gravity could greatly benefit human health.

➢ Extended exposure to low gravity environments like those on Mars has been shown to cause muscle atrophy, bone loss, cardiovascular deconditioning, and vision problems. In contrast, Venus' gravity at this altitude could help preserve muscle and bone strength, maintain cardiovascular function, and reduce risks associated with fluid redistribution and spaceflight-associated neuro-ocular syndrome (SANS). These benefits would simplify health protocols and allow for a more Earth-like living experience, potentially supporting long-term human presence in ways that Mars cannot.

➢ Radiation levels in this region of Venus's atmosphere also compare favourably to those on Earth—offering protection similar to places like Canada—whereas Mars, with its thin atmosphere and lack of magnetic field, exposes colonists to higher levels of harmful cosmic and solar radiation.

➤ These unique environmental advantages have led some visionaries to propose the idea of floating habitats in Venus's upper atmosphere. **NASA's HAVOC Project (High Altitude Venus Operational Concept** – see over) imagines dirigible-like airships that would suspend human explorers in this Earth-like zone, allowing for both scientific observation and potential long-term habitation. Admittedly, the presence of sulfuric acid in the atmosphere remains a formidable challenge, but one that might be overcome with specialized materials and protective coatings.

➤ **Oxygen and nitrogen** are **lighter than CO_2**, which dominates Venus's atmosphere, meaning a habitat or vessel filled with breathable air would naturally float — similar to helium in Earth's atmosphere.

➤ **Super-rotation winds** at that altitude would carry a floating habitat around the planet in about 4–5 Earth days, creating a relatively short and tolerable day/night cycle. Unlike the surface where about 1400 Earth hours of daylight are followed by 1400 hours of night, or 117 Earth days (precisely 116.75). This would be an extreme and challenging cycle for any surface operations or habitation.

➤ Any **extravehicular activity** would require **acid-resistant suits**, though they wouldn't need to be pressurized, since the pressure is already Earth-like at that altitude.

Image: NASA Langley Research Centre

➢ While Venus lacks water, colonists could potentially bring hydrogen and produce water through chemical processes, such as those used in fuel cells—further enabling a manageable environment. In this way, Venus may yet offer humanity a second home—one floating above the clouds, where conditions are unexpectedly, and intriguingly, like Earth.

Appendix G
Scientific Foundations

Appendix G explores the real-world astronomical research behind planetary orbital instability, including simulations by Jacques Laskar showing that rare but possible gravitational disturbances—particularly involving Mercury—could lead to chaotic changes in neighbouring planetary orbits.

Planetary Chaos and Orbital Instability

The stability of planetary orbits has long been assumed, yet recent high-precision simulations reveal that our solar system may not be permanently stable over astronomical timescales. Led by French astronomer Jacques Laskar, a series of studies have shown that small gravitational perturbations between planets, particularly those involving Mercury, can lead to chaotic orbital diffusion.

Laskar's 2008 research utilized more than 1000 simulations based on secular equations averaged over planetary orbits. The results demonstrated that Mercury's orbit could, in rare cases, become extremely elongated, or eccentric, with a 1–2% probability of exceeding an eccentricity of 0.6 within 5 billion years. In simulations excluding general relativity effects, Mercury's eccentricity exceeded 0.8 in less than 3 billion years in some cases, potentially placing it on a collision course with Venus or even Earth.

The chaotic behavior arises mainly from resonances between the perihelion precession rates of Jupiter and Mercury. When these rates align, even slightly, Jupiter's gravitational tugs on Mercury are amplified, increasing its orbital eccentricity. The simulations indicate that while such events are rare, they are statistically plausible and supported by numerical modeling.

Inner Planet Destabilization in Direct Simulations

In a follow-up 2009 study, Laskar and Gastineau performed 2500 direct numerical simulations of the solar system's evolution over 5 billion years. These simulations introduced tiny variations in Mercury's initial position—on the order of one metre—to explore sensitivity to initial conditions.

The outcome was startling: in about 1% of simulations, Mercury's orbit destabilized, leading to potential collisions with Venus or the Sun. In some cases, this orbital chaos triggered secondary disturbances in other terrestrial planets. One simulation showed Mars being ejected from the solar system; in another, Mars passed so close to Earth that tidal forces would likely have shredded it into fragments.

Summary and Implications for This Book

The scientific findings summarized here provide a plausible backdrop for the fictional events described in this book. While a planetary collision involving Venus is highly improbable in the near future, the underlying physics of gravitational resonance and chaotic orbital behavior are very real. These research efforts reinforce the idea that catastrophic planetary dynamics, though rare, are not outside the realm of scientific possibility.

References:

Laskar, J. (2008). Chaotic diffusion in the Solar System. IMCCE-CNRS, Observatoire de Paris. arXiv:0802.3371v1

Laskar, J., & Gastineau, M. (2009). Existence of collisional trajectories of Mercury, Mars and Venus with the Earth. Nature, 459, 817–819. DOI: 10.1038/nature08096

Battersby, S. (2009). Solar system's planets could spin out of control. New Scientist, 10 June 2009.

Appendix H
Image Credits and Attributions

Images featured throughout this book, particularly those relating to the Soviet Venera and Vega missions, are sourced from a range of public and archival collections. Unless otherwise noted, the following sources are credited:

- Lavochkin Association / Soviet Academy of Sciences – original Venera and Vega mission developers

- Roscosmos – the Russian space agency responsible for archiving and maintaining Soviet-era imagery

- NASA / NASA Planetary Photojournal – for cross-released or translated public domain images

  Don P. Mitchell – for restored and colour-processed Venera surface imagery (*www.mentallandscape.com*)

- Wikimedia Commons – where applicable, under appropriate Creative Commons or Public Domain licenses

- **Lyric Use Notice**
  The lyric excerpt *"I'm your Venus, I'm your fire, at your desire."* is quoted from the song *Venus*, written by **Robbie van Leeuwen** and performed by **Shocking Blue** (1969).
  It is used here for artistic and thematic purposes under fair use/fair dealing principles. All rights to the original work remain with the copyright holder.

Note: In cases where specific origin details were unavailable due to limited archival records, imagery has been included under good faith educational and documentary use, with attribution to the most reliable known source.

Author's Note

Over several millennia, Venus has continued to haunt the human imagination—initially as a goddess, but now also as a warning. Its brilliance once inspired songs of desire; its reality now compels respect. The very planet that lit up pop charts and ancient mythologies reminds us that celestial beauty can mask cataclysmic potential.

In the end, Venus is not merely a symbol—it is a stark warning of the possible future that may await our own Earth.

<u>Kosmos 482: The Venus Probe Coming Home</u>

In the spring of 1972, as the Cold War simmered and the Space Race surged forward, the Soviet Union launched Kosmos 482—a spacecraft meant to blaze a trail to Venus. It was part of the same ambitious engineering lineage that produced the Venera probes, those remarkable machines that gave humanity our first glimpses of Venus's hellish surface. But sometimes, even the best-laid plans go awry.

A critical malfunction in the upper stage of its Molniya rocket left Kosmos 482 stranded in a highly elliptical orbit around Earth, never reaching escape velocity to begin its intended journey toward our sister planet. The spacecraft broke into two parts: the main body and its Venus lander module—a half-ton metal sphere engineered to withstand the extreme conditions of Venus's atmosphere.

The main spacecraft fell back to Earth in 1981, but the lander—a testament to Soviet engineering—remained aloft in a slowly decaying orbit. This spherical module, measuring approximately 1 metre wide, was constructed from titanium alloy and equipped with thick ablative shielding. It carried no active propulsion system, simply continuing its lonely path around Earth while gradually being pulled closer by atmospheric drag.

In 2025—more than 53 years after its launch—Kosmos 482's lander finally began its long-anticipated return to Earth. Satellite tracker Marco Langbroek from Delft Technical University in the Netherlands was among the first to calculate its imminent re-entry, projecting the window to fall between May 8 and May 11. The world watched with a mixture of awe and curiosity as the old probe, long forgotten by many, made headlines once again.

Here's the extraordinary twist: because the lander was built to survive the infernal descent through Venus's dense, acidic atmosphere—far more hostile than Earth's—experts suspected it might actually endure the fiery plunge back through our skies intact.

And they were right.

On May 11, 2025, tracking agencies confirmed that the Kosmos 482 lander had re-entered Earth's atmosphere and splashed down in the remote waters of the southern Indian Ocean. The descent was swift, and the final moments likely went unwitnessed by human eyes—no radar-guided recovery, no camera footage, just the hiss of re-entry and the silent embrace of the sea.

Though it never reached Venus, the lander completed a different kind of odyssey—one that spanned generations, defied orbital decay, and ended not with destruction, but with a soft disappearance into the ocean's depths. It now rests beneath the waves, a cold and silent relic of an era when nations raced to other worlds with blueprints, ambition, and an iron will.

Kosmos 482 serves as a rare example of a Venus lander that never left home—and a reminder that space missions, even failed ones, can have remarkable and long-lived legacies.

Image: ESA

www.ingramcontent.com/pod-product-compliance
Lightning Source LLC
Chambersburg PA
CBHW07143826C626
47170CB00008B/2759